OUT OF
THE COLD

OUT OF THE COLD

A ROBYN HUNTER MYSTERY

NORAH McCLINTOCK

MINNEAPOLIS

First U.S. edition published in 2012 by Lerner Publishing Group, Inc.

Darby Creek
A division of Lerner Publishing Group, Inc.
241 First Avenue North
Minneapolis, MN 55401 U.S.A.

Website address: www.lernerbooks.com

The image in this book is used with the permission of:
Front cover: © Mika/CORBIS.

Main body text set in Janson Text Lt Std 11.5/15.
Typeface provided by Linotype AG.

Library of Congress Cataloging-in-Publication Data

McClintock, Norah.
    Out of the cold / by Norah McClintock.
       p.   cm. — (Robyn Hunter mysteries ; #4)
    ISBN: 978–0–7613–8314–7 (lib. bdg. : alk. paper)
    [1. Mystery and detective stories. 2. Homeless persons—
  Fiction. 3. Voluntarism—Fiction.] I. Title.
  PZ7.M478414184Ou 2012
  [Fic]—dc23   2011034339

Manufactured in the United States of America
1 – BP – 7/15/12

TO MR. JONES

CHAPTER **ONE**

My father's enormous loft was as silent as a mortuary and as dark as the inside of a coffin—except for the glow from his study. I walked toward it.

Staring out at me from the computer screen at my dad's desk was a not-quite-right likeness of Ted Gold, the man my mother had been seeing for almost a year. My parents are divorced. Despite my mother's best efforts to keep her personal life, well, *personal*, my father is well aware of Ted. He'd even met him a couple of times—*not* my mother's idea. I stared at the Ted-like picture on the screen and wondered what my father was up to. Knowing him, probably nothing my mother would approve of.

Somewhere else in the loft, something hit the floor with a bang.

I jumped. "Dad?"

I poked my head out of his study just in time to see someone—a woman I had never seen before—picking a heavy hardcover book up from the floor. She was wearing a bathrobe and had a towel wound around her head. She didn't look anywhere near as surprised to see me as I was to see her.

"You must be Robyn," she said, smiling. "Mac was hoping to be here when you arrived, but he called to say that he was running late." That was typical of my father. He has made a career out of being late for every type of occasion, from school concerts to wedding anniversary celebrations, which helps explain why he and my mother are no longer married. "He asked me to tell you he should be home by nine." She glanced at the clock on the mantelpiece. "Uh-oh. If I don't get going, *I'm* going to be late." She disappeared into what was supposed to be *my* room, but which my dad also uses as a guest room. "Nice to meet you," she said as she closed the door.

Meet me? She hadn't even told me her name.

Okay, so a woman I had never seen before (an awfully *young* woman, considering that my father was firmly in his forties) had taken a shower, or maybe a bath, in my father's bathroom and was getting dressed in my (part-time) bedroom. What was a girl supposed to do in an awkward (for me, if not for her) situation like this?

I decided to bail. I left my suitcase near the front door where I had dropped it and went downstairs to see if Nick was around.

I hadn't seen Nick in seven days—and before that, I hadn't seen him alone, just the two of us, in weeks. My mother claimed that she had nothing against Nick personally, but that didn't mean she considered him ideal boyfriend material for me. Nick has had a few problems, some of them with the law. He also didn't have what my mother would consider the best family situation. Both of his parents are dead. His stepfather and stepbrother are both in prison. Nick is supposed to be living with his aunt, but that didn't work out—Nick didn't get along with his aunt's new boyfriend. So for the last couple of months he'd been renting an apartment from my father, who owns a building that used to be a carpet factory. My father lives on the top floor. The first floor is occupied by a trendy gourmet restaurant called La Folie. The second floor consists of six apartments. Nick lives in one of them. My mother has never been comfortable with that. She was much, much less comfortable after what had happened last month, before I went on a weeklong school trip.

"You were almost killed," she'd said. "And it was all Nick's fault."

It wasn't *all* Nick's fault, but there was no point in arguing with my mother. And I hadn't been killed. Everything had worked out just fine. But that hadn't stopped my mother from having a total meltdown. She forbade me to see Nick ever again. She ordered my father to evict him and was furious when he refused. "Fine," she'd said. "Robyn is not setting foot in that building as long as that boy is there." I argued with her until I almost lost my voice. In the end, it was Ted who negotiated a compromise—basically, a month of extremely limited access that broke down like this: I wasn't allowed to see Nick or even talk to him for a whole week. For two weeks after that, I could only see him in my mother's or Ted's presence. Nick had been so uncomfortable after the first time that mostly we had just talked on the phone. Who could blame him? My mother had allowed him to come over to her house to watch a movie with me and then had sat in one corner of the room the whole time—reading, supposedly. I had hoped my father would cut us some slack. He hadn't. Other than refusing to evict Nick, he had gone along with my mother. He didn't want to make waves. "Your mom has every right to be upset," he'd said.

For the final week, I was out of town. My mother had looked relieved when she saw me off on the bus.

But, at long last, my punishment was over. I could see Nick whenever I wanted—without a chaperone. I couldn't wait. I had called him a couple of times while I was out of town, but he hadn't answered his phone. He'd probably been working. Nick put in a lot of hours at a part-time job. He also went to school. That didn't leave him with a lot of spare time.

My heart was pounding as I knocked on his door.

There was no answer.

I knocked again.

Still no answer. He wasn't home.

I heard footsteps in the stairwell. Nick? But no, instead of coming up from street level, the footsteps were coming down from the third floor. Must have been the mystery woman from my father's place. I waited in the second-floor hallway until I heard the door on the ground floor swoosh open and clang shut again. Then I went down to La Folie. Nick had landed a job there (thanks to my father) right after he had supposedly almost got me killed and shortly after he had broken his ankle. He was probably in La Folie's kitchen, perched on a stool, scraping plates and loading them into the industrial dishwasher.

.   .   .

"Isn't Nick working today?" I asked Lauren, the hostess.

She gave me a funny look. "No," she said. "He isn't." I was pretty sure she was going to say something else, but just then a party of six came through the door. "Excuse me, Robyn," she said as she bustled away.

If Nick wasn't at home and he wasn't at work, maybe he was visiting his aunt. Or maybe he was just out. I went back up to my father's place and lugged my suitcase to my room. I'll say one thing for the mystery woman— she was neat. Everything was exactly as I had left it. You would never have known that she'd been there at all. I was on my way to the kitchen to make a cup of tea when I heard the door. It was my father. His face lit up when he saw me.

"Robbie! How was the trip?" he said. "Did you have a good time?"

I had spent the past week on what my school had billed as a cultural field trip, but there had been no fields involved. This trip had been decidedly urban—three days of lectures and hands-on learning at a museum, two days of educational sightseeing, and an evening at the theatre. My best friend Morgan had gone too, and we had been rooming together, which meant, "I had a pretty good time, Dad."

My father was still smiling while he looked around. "Where's—"

"She said she had to run. Who is she, anyway?"

"Tara?"

So that was her name.

"You hungry?" my father said as he hung up his coat. "Because I'm starving."

"I'm fine." I followed him into the kitchen and took a seat at the counter while he rummaged around in the fridge. "So who exactly is she?"

Out came a chunk of cheese—extra-old cheddar, I think—and the end of a ham, followed by a jar of Dijon mustard, a tomato, half a loaf of dark bread, and a container of coleslaw.

"Sorry, did you say something, Robbie?"

"Tara—who is she?"

"She's a very old friend," he said, smiling. There was a twinkle in his eye that made me think he wasn't telling me everything.

"She doesn't look that old," I said. "In fact, she seems kind of young."

"Does she?" He pulled a knife from the drawer and sliced up the tomato. "I think she's just about right." He rinsed the knife and cut into the cheese. "Are you sure you're not hungry?"

"I'm sure. How long have you known her?"

"Long enough, I guess." He pulled out another knife and used it to spread a slice of bread with a thin layer of mustard. "Did you tell your mother you're back?"

"I called her as soon as the bus got in." Which reminded me. "Have you been snooping on Ted?"

He looked confused. Or maybe he was just *acting* confused. With my father, it's sometimes hard to tell.

"What do you mean?" he said.

"I saw a picture of him on your computer. Have you been checking up on him?" It wouldn't have surprised me. For some reason that I didn't quite understand, especially given how rough the divorce had been, my father still seems to be in love with my mother. It would be just like him to try to dig up some dirt on Ted. Well, good luck. Ted is a sweet, mild-mannered, all-round nice guy. If he had any secrets, they were more likely to be along the lines of anonymous donations to good causes than scandals or indiscretions.

"Checking up on him? Why would I do that?" my father said. He had been layering ham, cheese, and tomato onto the mustardy bread, but he stopped and looked me in the eye to show that he was innocent of any wrongdoing.

The thing is, though, my father is pretty good at deceit. He's the first to admit that it's often necessary in his line of work. He had been a police officer for nearly twenty years. These days he runs his own private security and investigations business. He says that sometimes, if you want to get the truth out of a liar, you have to lie yourself. My mother sees it differently. She says that lying comes as naturally to my father as breathing does to the rest of the world. "I promised your mom that I wouldn't snoop into her affairs," he said. "And I keep my word."

Uh-huh. I studied him for a moment, trying to decide if he actually expected me to believe that. Then he said, "Robyn, about Nick—"

"I was going to ask you about him," I said. "I went to look for him, but he wasn't home and he's not at work. I thought for sure he'd be here. Have you seen him?"

"You went downstairs?"

"Yeah, but he wasn't there."

"Did you talk to Fred?"

He meant Fred Smith, owner of La Folie.

"No, but I talked to Lauren," I said.

"What did she say?"

"That Nick wasn't working today." Wait a minute. "Did you just call me Robyn?" The last time my father had called me by my proper name instead of using my nickname was when he'd told me about the divorce. "Is something wrong? Did something happen to Nick?"

My father dropped the top piece of bread onto his sandwich.

"I wish I knew," he said. He cut the sandwich in half, carried it and the container of coleslaw over to the counter, and sat down opposite me. "I haven't seen him since you left for that school trip."

"What do you mean, you haven't seen him? You mean he hasn't been home?"

My father laid a hand on my shoulder.

"Dad, where's Nick?"

"I don't know."

"What do you mean, you don't know?"

"He's gone, Robbie. I don't know where. I don't know why. I don't even know exactly when he left. All I know is, he's gone."

. . .

"Gone?" Morgan said at school the next day. "What do you mean, he's gone?"

"I mean, he's not here. He's someplace else."

"Someplace else *where?*"

That was the million-dollar question. I told Morgan everything I knew, which wasn't much. Two days before we got back from our trip, my father had been downstairs having lunch at La Folie. After he ate, he went back to the kitchen to say hi to Nick, but Nick wasn't there. When my father asked Fred Smith how Nick was doing, Fred told him that Nick didn't work there anymore.

"Did he get fired?" Morgan said.

"He quit." Fred had told my father that Nick was nice about it. He thanked Fred for giving him a job and apologized for leaving on such short notice.

"He didn't say why he was quitting?" Morgan said.

I looked grimly at Morgan. "He said he was going out of town."

"Why? For how long?"

"Fred didn't ask, and Nick didn't say."

"What about your dad? Didn't Nick say anything to him?"

I shook my head. "My dad checked Nick's apartment after he talked to Fred. Most of Nick's things are gone." He'd left his furniture, almost all of which my father had given to him, and the few kitchen things he owned—dishes, a couple of pots, all bought at thrift stores—but he had taken his clothes and his more personal possessions.

"I don't get it," Morgan said. "Why didn't he call you and tell you where he was going?"

I had asked myself the same question a hundred times.

"Didn't he even leave a note?" Morgan said. "You don't think he's in trouble, do you?"

All I could do was shrug. Then I said what had been on my mind all night. "Morgan, what if he left because he didn't think he had any reason to stay?"

"What do you mean?"

"He's not getting along with his aunt. Joey's in prison." Joey was Nick's stepbrother. "Angie and the baby don't live here anymore." Angie was Joey's girlfriend.

She had recently had a baby boy. "And he wasn't allowed to see me unless my mom or Ted was right there with us. What if he got fed up?" Nick had had problems controlling his anger in the past. I was pretty sure he resented the way my mother had been treating him. Maybe he'd decided that putting up with her just to be with me wasn't worth it. Or maybe—I hated to think about it—maybe he'd met someone else.

"He knows you were away." Morgan said. "He knows when you were supposed to be back. If he cares about you, Robyn, he'll call."

If he cared so much, why hadn't he told me he was leaving? Why hadn't he called me already?

.   .   .

I got the key to Nick's apartment from my father and checked the place myself after school. Apart from a film of dust that had accumulated since he'd left, the place was spotless. I looked for a note but didn't find one. I even checked under the furniture in case it had fallen behind a dresser or under a table. Nothing. He was really gone.

I called Nick's Aunt Beverly and asked if she knew where he was.

"Why?" she said. "He isn't in trouble again, is he? Don't tell me he got fired from another job."

He obviously hadn't told her he was leaving, either. I said that I had been out of town and that I was trying to track him down. I didn't have the heart to say anything else.

I went to the group home where Nick had been living when I first met him. It was for kids who had been sentenced to open custody—no locks, no bars, just strict discipline, lots of chores, and programs in life skills and anger management. Nick had at least one friend there, a guy named Antoine, whom I'd met during the summer. Maybe he knew where Nick was.

"Sorry," the woman who answered the door told me. "Antoine isn't here anymore."

"Do you know where I can find him?"

"I'm afraid I'm not at liberty to give out that information."

Judging by her somber expression, wherever Antoine was, *he* wasn't at liberty. Otherwise she would have told me.

For the next couple of days, I jumped every time my cell phone or the phone at my mom's house rang. When my mother finally said, "For heaven's sake, Robyn, relax," I burst into tears. My mother gave me a sympathetic look. She said she was sorry that Nick had taken off without a word. She said she understood how I must feel. She was trying to be nice, but I couldn't help thinking that she was relieved that Nick was out of my life. Then she said the very last thing that I wanted to hear. She said, "Maybe it's for the best."

. . .

"I still don't understand," I said. "Should I have done something different? Should I have snuck out to see him?" My mother would have grounded me for life if she'd found out I'd done that.

"It was only a few weeks, Robyn," Morgan said. "It wasn't exactly the end of the world. And you said you talked to him on the phone almost every day before the trip."

"I thought if we did what my mom wanted, she would see that he was okay. I was more worried about what she thought than about what Nick thought."

I didn't mean to cry again, especially not in the school cafeteria where everyone could see me. But every time I thought about Nick, tears rose up all over again. Why had he taken off? Why hadn't he told me where he was going?

"What if something has happened to him? What if he's met someone else? What if—?"

Morgan pulled a wad of tissues out of her purse and handed them to me.

"I like Nick," she said. "You know I do."

In fact, I didn't know that. I knew she thought he was good-looking, which he is—tall and lean, with jet-black hair and startling purple-blue eyes. I knew she thought he was exciting and kind of dangerous—mostly because of all the trouble he had been in and because of the hairline scar that runs from the bridge of his nose to the bottom of his right ear. It makes him look like the kind of person who doesn't shy away from a fight. And it's true. He doesn't. I also knew that she respected the fact that I liked him, a *lot*. But I didn't know that she actually liked him.

"But," she said—the word I had been waiting for—"you haven't known him for very long, which means that you may not know him as well as you think you do."

"What are you saying, Morgan?"

"There could be a dozen reasons he left. Till you hear from him, there's nothing you can do. You just have to wait."

"For how long?"

"I don't know." She squeezed my hand. "But I do know that whatever happens, it's not your fault. You didn't do anything wrong. If he wasn't prepared to wait a couple of weeks for you, that's his problem, not yours. I also know that if worse comes to worst, you can't keep crying over him. And don't give me that look, Robyn. You know what I mean. It's been almost a whole week since we got back."

"Hey, guys," a cheery male voice said. I looked up. It was Billy Royal, my other best friend in the whole world and, recently, Morgan's boyfriend. He slipped an arm around Morgan and kissed her on the cheek before dropping into the empty chair beside her. "What's up?"

"Robyn is still beating herself up over Nick's disappearance," Morgan said, as if I were doing something wrong.

Billy gave me a sympathetic look. "Still haven't heard from him, huh?"

I shook my head.

"She needs to get her mind off him," Morgan said.

"I don't *want* to get my mind off him," I said. "I want to know where he is and why he left."

"What I mean is, you need to get your mind off thinking about him *all the time*," Morgan said. "It'll drive you crazy. You need to get busy with something."

"Why don't you come to the homeless shelter with Morgan and me?" Billy said. "They can always use extra help."

Billy volunteered at a place for the homeless. He also volunteered at an animal rights organization and at the Humane Society, and was a founder of and the most active member in the Downtown Avian Rescue Club, which rescued injured migratory birds. Needless to say, he's a vegan.

"I don't know," I said. I admire Billy, but the way I was feeling, I thought I'd probably just depress the destitute.

"Seriously, Robyn, you should try it," Billy said. "The best way I know to feel good about yourself is to help someone else. Isn't that right, Morgan?"

Morgan nodded. "Although, to be honest," she said, "I feel just fine about myself."

I was sure that was true. Morgan was not given to self-doubt, self-pity, self-loathing or, especially, self-criticism. The person who liked Morgan best was Morgan herself. Billy was her number-two admirer.

"We're going down there tomorrow, right, Morgan?" Billy said. "And I know they're looking for more volunteers. The colder it gets, the more people use the shelter." It was really cold already, and the nights getting longer. It was dark by five in the afternoon. "They need as many people as they can get to make soup and sandwiches, set out coffee, clean up after meals, sort and hand out donations of warm clothing and sleeping bags—stuff like that. It'll make you feel better. And you'll meet a lot of interesting people. What do you say?"

I wanted to say no. I didn't feel like doing anything. But Billy made it sound as if I'd be welcomed with open arms, so instead I agreed.

Billy beamed at me. "It's a great place to volunteer, Robyn. You won't regret it."

As it turned out, he was wrong. It wasn't long before I was sorry I had ever said yes.

CHAPTER **TWO**

The way we had arranged it: I would meet Morgan and Billy at the shelter, Billy would introduce me to the director, and the director would assign me something to do.

The change in plans: While I was waiting for the bus, Morgan called me on my cell phone and said she couldn't make it after all because she had woken up with a really bad sore throat. She said they didn't like people to volunteer at the shelter if they were even remotely sick—a lot of the homeless people who used the place weren't in the best of health. Some of them had immune systems that were seriously unreliable. But, she said, Billy was on his way, he was excited that I was going to join him, and he was dying to show me around.

The way it actually happened: I got off the bus where Billy had told me to. I could have waited for a second bus, but it wasn't due for another ten minutes. It wouldn't take that long to walk to the homeless shelter, and walking would help me to stay warm. At first I was moving past downtown stores, office buildings, and restaurants. Even there I kept running into people who were down and out. I'd only gone half a block before a grubby young man sitting in the doorway of a vacant store asked me for money. He was half-wrapped in a weathered sleeping bag and he kept his eyes on the ground when I dropped some quarters into a plastic cup on the sidewalk in front of him. One block onward, I passed a man with one leg who was leaning against a utility pole. He was holding out an empty margarine container and muttering, "Sparechangesparechangesparechange," over and over in a whispery voice. I shrugged apologetically. I had already given all my coins to the young guy in the doorway.

On the next block, an old guy sitting in front of an office building was cursing at a well-dressed man who was digging into his pocket for his wallet. He dropped a five-dollar bill into an upturned hat on the sidewalk, but it didn't silence the old man. He kept right on cursing. I glanced at him and gasped involuntarily when he looked up at me. A jagged red scar slashed through his left eyebrow and ended halfway down his cheek. His left eye looked twisted. When I stared at him, wondering if he was blind in that eye, he started to curse at me too. The well-dressed man gave me a sympathetic look before he turned and walked away. I picked up my pace and wondered what had made Billy and Morgan think this would cheer me up.

The scenery changed rapidly after that, and I soon found myself in depressing surroundings. The shelter was located in a run-down part of the city a couple of blocks away from a sprawling low-income housing project. Just as I was about to turn the corner, a woman in a puffy coat and tattered sneakers started screaming at me. At least, that's what I thought she was doing. It turned out that she was just plain screaming—it had nothing to do with me. She shoved past me, pushing a shopping cart heaped with what looked like garbage, shouting and cursing and looking ferocious.

I arrived at my destination five minutes early. Even though the temperature was well below zero and the sky was a gloomy lead-gray, a loose group of men in grime-encrusted coats, most of them with dirty hair and scraggly beards, crowded the sidewalk in front of the church hall that housed the shelter. At first I couldn't figure out why they were standing out in the icy cold when they could have been inside where it was warm. Then I noticed that almost all of them were smoking. Billy had told me that the shelter enforced a strict no-smoking policy, so people who wanted a cigarette had to go outside. A couple of them gave me a once-over as I made my way to the door. One of them said something I didn't quite catch to a second man, and the second man responded with a laugh that was as crusty as his coat.

I opened the door, stepped inside, and was immediately overwhelmed by the heat and by the stench of unwashed bodies and tobacco that mingled with the aromas of coffee and food cooking. I had never smelled anything quite like it. I was surprised that Morgan hadn't said something about it. There was no way *she* would have gotten used to it.

From what I could see from the main entrance, the shelter took up the whole church hall and consisted of one enormous room that had been divided into several areas, as well as a kitchen—which I spotted when someone bustled through a door on the far side of the hall—and several smaller rooms.

I looked around the large main room. In the area farthest from the entrance, some battered armchairs and two sagging couches sat around a television set that was tuned to a talk show. Most of the seats were occupied. A few people, mostly women, each with a bundle buggy parked nearby, were staring at the screen. A few others appeared to be asleep.

Another part of the room was set up with a long wooden table and folding chairs. People sat hunched over orange plastic trays that held bowls of cereal, mugs of coffee, and plates of toast. Along one wall, a woman—a volunteer?—was handing out plastic-wrapped sandwiches and containers of soup. Coffee was self-serve from a huge urn set up on another, smaller table.

The third area consisted of a half-dozen card tables ringed with folding chairs, some raggedy armchairs, and a small bookshelf that was crammed with paperback books. Decks of cards, a couple of cribbage boards, and some chess and checker sets sat atop the shelf. A group of men sat around one of the tables, playing cards.

I didn't see Billy anywhere.

A hand fell on my shoulder and I jumped. I turned and looked into the weathered face of a man in faded jeans and a frayed denim shirt. His long gray hair was pulled back into a ponytail. He smelled of soap and aftershave lotion.

"You look lost," he said.

"I'm looking for Billy Royal," I said. "I'm supposed to meet him here."

The man smiled. "You must be Robyn. Billy called. I'm afraid he's had a change of plans. I'm Art Donovan. I run this place." He thrust out a hand and we shook. "Are you handy in the kitchen?"

I nodded.

"Great. I'll have someone show you around. Then, if you don't mind, I'll put you to work in the kitchen." He raised an arm and snapped his fingers. "Ben!" he called. "Ben, over here."

One of the card players, younger and better dressed than the others, got up and loped toward us.

"Robyn, this is Ben Logan," Art said. "Ben, meet Robyn . . ."

"Hunter," I said, supplying my last name.

"Robyn is here for the day," Art said. "Who knows, maybe she'll like it so much that she'll decide to come back. Do me a favor. Show her around. Then take her in to Betty." He smiled at me. "Betty can always use an extra hand. Welcome aboard, Robyn." He left me with Ben.

Ben looked me over.

"Nice boots," he said.

I glanced down at my feet. "Thanks," I said. They were brand new and I loved them. My mother had really grumbled about the price.

"Nice jacket too," Ben said. It was also new, and amazingly warm. "Looks expensive." He made it sound like that was a bad thing. His eyes shifted to the gold earrings my father had given me for my birthday and then to my new sweater.

Like Art Donovan, Ben was wearing faded blue jeans. He also had on a pullover sweater that had seen better days and a pair of beat-up sneakers. I started to feel self-conscious. Compared to him—to everyone in the place—I was seriously overdressed.

"Come on, I'll give you the grand tour," he said. The look on his face made me think that he would rather be scrubbing toilets. First he showed me where the various offices were—one for Art Donovan right off the main hall, one for a nurse who came by regularly, and, down a short hallway, one for a social worker who helped people get the things they needed. There was also a workspace with a couple of computers that visitors to the shelter could use to access the Internet. Then he led me to the far end of the room, where a cooking show had come on the TV. Nobody was talking anymore.

Ben nudged me over beside the TV and said, in a loud voice, "Hey, everyone, this is Robyn."

A couple of people pulled their eyes away from the TV just long enough to give me a once-over. The rest of them remained focused on the cooking show.

Next he led me to the long table where a dozen or so people spooned up milky oatmeal. One man was dunking pieces of toast into a mug of coffee and—yuck!—sucking on them.

"Hey, everyone," Ben said again, "this is Robyn." A few pairs of eyes looked from breakfast to me. One of them was the scruffy young man I'd given money to in front of the vacant store. His hands were wrapped around a mug of coffee. He stared at my boots and frowned when Ben introduced me. Ben shrugged at the lack of response. "You can see how excited everyone is to meet a brand new two-four," he said.

"A two-four?" I said.

"As in twenty-four—hours. One-day wonders. We get them around here all the time. Kids who have to put in a few hours of community service for school. People who drop by once a year, usually to serve Christmas dinner, so that their consciences won't bother them too much for having scored some Gucci or Prada or Louis Vuitton on Christmas morning. Come on, I'll show you the rest of the place, so you can tell your friends what a shelter for the homeless looks like."

I stared at him. "Where do you get off talking to me like that?" I said. "You don't know anything about me."

He looked me over again, staring pointedly at my earrings, my jacket, my boots.

"I get it," I said. "You think that because of the way I dress"—I looked just as pointedly at his own shabby attire—"I don't care about these people. Is that it?"

As soon as I said "these people," a few people looked up at me from coffee mugs and cereal bowls. Great.

"Is that why you're here?" he said. "Because you care so much?"

I wished I could say that that was exactly why I was there, but it wasn't. There was no way I was going to admit that to him, though. "I'm here because my friend Billy volunteers here and he told me they're always looking for more help," I said stiffly.

"Billy?" He sounded surprised. "Billy Royal?"

I nodded.

"*You're* a friend of Billy's?" He looked as if he'd just witnessed Billy sinking his teeth into a thick, juicy steak.

"Since kindergarten," I said.

"Hey, I'm sorry. I didn't know. I thought you were—"

"A one-day wonder. Yeah. I got that. Mr. Donovan said they could use some help in the kitchen, so if you'll excuse me . . ." *And even if you won't*, I thought. I turned, went into the kitchen, and introduced myself to a woman who turned out to be Betty. She was standing in front of a counter, shelling what looked like several dozen hard-boiled eggs. A huge pot of soup simmered on the stove beside her.

"Can you follow a recipe?" she said, gesturing to a binder on the counter.

"We do three kinds of cookies—oatmeal raisin, chocolate chip, and molasses spice. I need twelve dozen of each."

"Twelve *dozen*?"

"Of each."

"But that makes . . ." My math failed me.

"Four hundred and thirty-two cookies. That should get us through the weekend."

Four hundred and thirty-two cookies would get them through the weekend?

"It would be a lot easier to just buy them," Betty said, reading my mind. "But these people don't eat right unless they're *given* good food. That includes cookies made with real eggs—without all those chemicals and preservatives they put in the store-bought stuff. We get between eighty and one hundred people in here for dinner every day. Each person gets a piece of fruit and two cookies for dessert. That's one hundred and sixty to two hundred cookies per dinner. We also package some up to give to people who want to take a sandwich with them instead. And there are always people who sneak a few extras. The pans are there." She pointed. "Bowls, wooden spoons, measuring cups, and measuring spoons are all in there." She pointed to the far side of the room. "We can get twelve good-sized cookies on a pan, two pans in the oven at a time, fifteen minutes per batch."

That made . . . my math skills failed me again.

"That means four and a half hours just to bake the cookies. But first you have to mix the dough. Here's what you do . . ."

What you did, it turned out, was mix one batch of cookie dough—I started with oatmeal raisin—and scoop it out onto cookie sheets. Then, between popping batches of the first kind of cookie into the oven and taking them out again, I mixed up the second batch of cookie dough. Et cetera.

.   .   .

Two and a half hours and a mountain of cookies later, Betty said she was going outside for a smoke.

"Yeah, I know smoking isn't good for me," she said. "You have any idea how many times I've tried to quit? Mind the store for me, huh?" She pulled on a parka. "Clients aren't allowed in the kitchen. And absolutely *no one* is allowed into the basement." She nodded to the door that led downstairs.

"Why don't you just keep it locked?" I said.

"All of my supplies are down there," she said. "And Art's the only one who has a key. He says it's easier to control access that way. He unlocks the door when I come in and locks it again as soon as I'm finished for the day. Strictly off-limits to clients. I'll be back in ten minutes."

I had just started to mix the molasses cookie dough when a raggedy old man shuffled into the room. At first I stared at his head. It was lopsided, as if somewhere under his matted hair a piece of his skull was missing. Then I looked at his face—at the scar and the twisted left eye—and realized he was the same man I had seen out on the street, shouting at the man who had dropped a five-dollar bill into his hat.

Betty had told me that the kitchen was off-limits to people who used the shelter—she called them clients. "If anyone comes in, politely ask them to leave," she had said. "If they won't leave, call Art."

The old man looked at the oatmeal raisin cookies that were sitting in big plastic containers on the counters. I watched him and hoped that he would go away.

Instead, he started stuffing his pockets with cookies.

"Excuse me," I said, "but I don't think you're allowed to do that."

He stuffed more cookies into his pockets.

"*Excuse me*," I said again. I was thinking about all of the people who came to the shelter for dinner every day. They probably looked forward to their cookies. "Sorry, but you can't take those."

I started toward him—and stopped abruptly when he spun around to face me, his fists raised like a boxer. At first I thought it was kind of funny—this old man trying to scare me so that he could grab some cookies, just like a little kid. Then I saw the wild look in his eyes.

He kept his fists up and stared belligerently at me. Then he took a step toward me.

I backed away. As soon as I did, he shuffled over to the counter on the other side of the kitchen where

Betty had been cutting sandwiches in half and wrapping them in plastic. The knife she had been using was lying on a cutting board next to a bowl of shelled hardboiled eggs. The old man's hand edged toward it. I glanced around frantically. Where was Betty? She must have finished her cigarette. She'd know how to handle this.

The kitchen door opened. But it wasn't Betty. It was Ben Logan.

"Look, I've been thinking—" He looked from me to the old man, who had grabbed not the knife but a hardboiled egg, and was stuffing it whole into his mouth. Ben shook his head. "Mr. Duffy, you're not supposed to be in here," he said patiently. He walked up to the old man and touched his arm. "Come on. Let's get you out of here before Betty comes back. You know what she's like when she finds people in her kitchen who aren't supposed to be here."

Ben tugged on Mr. Duffy's arm. I flinched as I pictured the old man whirling around and punching him in the nose or, worse, grabbing the knife. But instead, Mr. Duffy allowed Ben to lead him to the kitchen door. Before they got there, Betty came through the door, unbuttoning her jacket. She shook her head when she saw the old man.

"What have you been up to, Mr. Duffy?" she said. When he didn't answer, she glanced at Ben, who merely shrugged. "Do I have to go through your pockets, Mr. Duffy?" Betty said.

Mr. Duffy stared at the floor. He didn't protest—he didn't even move—when Betty thrust a hand into one of his pockets.

"Mr. Duffy," she said, sounding as patient as Ben had, "you've been coming here long enough to know that there are only enough cookies to go around if everyone takes no more than his fair share." She pulled cookies out of one coat pocket and then another, and put them on the counter in a small heap. She shook her head again.

"That's sixteen cookies, Mr. Duffy. Do you know what Mr. Donovan would do if he found out you'd taken sixteen cookies?"

Mr. Duffy raised his head to look directly at her. He no longer seemed dangerous. He smiled, almost as if he were trying to charm her. It worked. She sighed, gave him two cookies—one oatmeal raisin and one chocolate chip—and said, "Go along with Ben. And Ben? There's no need to mention this to anyone, okay?"

Ben nodded. Mr. Duffy followed him out of the kitchen.

"What *would* Mr. Donovan do if he found out?" I said.

"He'd probably bar him from the shelter for a couple of days," Betty said. "Art tries to be understanding. We all do. Most of the people who use our services have a lot of problems, but most of them are reasonably well behaved. A few, however, sometimes act impulsively." From the way Betty had spoken to Mr. Duffy, I guessed he fit into the latter group. "There are two things we can't put up with—theft of shelter property, and violence. Everyone knows the rules and everyone knows why the rules are important." She looked at the cookies she had confiscated and, with a sigh, swept them into the garbage. "It's a waste, I know. Once he'd taken them, we might just as well have let him keep them, for all the good they'll do anyone else. But rules are rules, and it's not fair to let one person get away with raiding the kitchen."

.   .   .

"Is there anything else I can do?" I said after I had packed the last cookie into one of the huge plastic bins Betty had set out.

"I'd say you've done more than enough for one day," Betty said. "You must be tired."

She was right. My feet hurt and my back ached from standing for hours. I washed my hands one final time, hung up my apron, and went to look for my jacket. I stopped on my way out to say goodbye to Art Donovan.

"Thanks for your help today, Robyn," he said. "I hope Betty didn't work you too hard."

"I'm glad I could help," I said. But I was already picturing myself soaking in a deep, hot bubble bath. "Billy is always saying that you need more volunteers."

"Billy's right," Art said. "In fact, I don't suppose you'd have any free time tomorrow?"

"Well, I . . ." I didn't have any *definite* plans.

"We'll have more volunteers than we can handle come Christmas," he said. "But right now we're really shorthanded. There are a couple of people who usually help Betty in the kitchen, but one of them is out of town on a family emergency and the other one can't make it in either. What do you say?"

What could I say? I find it next to impossible to refuse when someone asks me for a favor.

"Terrific," Art said. "Wait a minute." He disappeared into a small office. When he returned, he handed me a sheet of paper. "Fill this out and bring it back with you tomorrow," he said. "It's a volunteer information form. We ask all volunteers to fill one out—basic personal information, who we should contact in case of emergency, that kind of thing. Okay?"

I nodded.

"Great," he said. "We'll see you tomorrow, then."

Twenty-four hours later, I was promising myself that I would learn how to say no.

CHAPTER THREE

Billy was busy with his animal rights organization the next day, so he couldn't go to the homeless shelter. Morgan was still sick—at least, that's what she told me in a whispery, poor-me-I've-got-a-sore-throat voice. So once again I headed downtown alone. And, wouldn't you know it, the first person I saw when I entered the church hall was Ben Logan. He was talking to the scruffy young guy I'd given money to. The guy pointed at me and said something to Ben, then put his hand up to cover his mouth. I could tell he was laughing. Ben laughed too and handed him something. I felt my cheeks burn. As I passed them, Ben said, "I didn't think you'd be back."

"I know," I said, without stopping. "You thought I was a two-four." I went directly into the kitchen, where Betty put me to work making and wrapping sandwiches. Ben showed up a few minutes later. I ignored him.

"Hey, come on," he said. "You not going to talk to me?"

"I saw you laughing at me," I said.

"Laughing at you?" He gave me a baffled look.

"Just now," I said. "With that other guy."

"We weren't laughing at you."

"He pointed at me."

"He pointed at your boots."

Again with the boots. "He doesn't like them either, huh?"

"He didn't say," Ben said. "But they're how he recognized you."

"What? What are you talking about?"

"Andrew never makes eye contact when he's asking for change. But he knows his footwear. Yesterday, when I was showing you around, he recognized your boots. He says you gave him money."

"And?" I said.

"And what?"

"What's so funny about my boots?"

"Nothing."

"You both laughed."

"True. But Andrew wasn't laughing at you. He was laughing at *me*."

"At you?" Did he actually expect me to believe that? Ben shifted awkwardly.

"Andrew told me yesterday that I'm more prejudiced than some of the people who pass him on the street. He said they judge him by how he looks and that I did the same thing to you. He bet me that you weren't a two-four and that you'd be back."

"He did?"

Ben nodded.

"And he was right. Andrew enjoys being right. That's why he was laughing. Look, I'm sorry about the way I acted. I didn't know you were a friend of Billy's. And it's obvious you're not a two-four. At the very least, you're a four-eight." He grinned. When I just stared at him, he said, "Get it?"

"I get it," I said.

"So what do you say? Friends?"

After the way he had treated me?

"Okay, I guess I deserve that," he said. "I was kind of obnoxious."

"Kind of?"

"I thought . . . well, you already know what I thought. If we can't be friends, can we at least agree not to be enemies? That way I might have a shot at convincing you what a great guy I really am."

Well, he was trying hard enough. And not only did he seem sincere, but he wasn't afraid to admit he was wrong. And it was obvious he thought highly of Billy. I relented just a little.

"I guess I could live with that," I said.

His face lit up, and I began to think he might not be so bad after all.

. . .

An hour later, I had made a couple dozen loaves' worth of sandwiches—egg, peanut butter, tuna—and I was about to start on some ham and cheese when Betty was summoned to a meeting with Art Donovan.

A few minutes later after she'd left, while I was spreading mustard on the bread I had laid out on the counter, someone darted through the kitchen door and disappeared into the basement.

I hesitated for a moment. Betty had told me that no one was allowed in the basement. I went to the top of the stairs.

"Hello?" I called. "Betty, is that you?"

No answer.

I heard a metallic *clunk* from somewhere down below. It sounded like someone was stacking cans of food. It had to be Betty. But why hadn't she answered? I started down the stairs. When I got to the bottom, I saw a man in a long, tattered overcoat, kneeling at the shelves that covered a wall. Mr. Duffy. He was burrowing into a cardboard box.

"Excuse me," I said. After the previous day, I was a little afraid of him, so I stood well back. "You're not supposed to be down here."

Duffy ignored me. He dipped into the box and started pulling out cans of peaches. He stuffed two into each of his coat pockets. I told myself to be understanding. He was homeless, and he was obviously hungry. But so was everyone else who used the shelter. Stealing from the storeroom was the same as stealing from all of the people who relied on the shelter for meals. It was against the rules. And hadn't Betty said that rules were rules? I remembered how she had handled the situation the day before. She had been patient, but firm.

"Mr. Duffy," I said, approaching him slowly. "You can't take those."

Duffy didn't react to me the way he had to Betty. He jumped to his feet and whirled around to face me. The expression on his scarred face was hostile.

"Mr. Duffy, please," I said. It was all I had the chance to say. He looked at me, then at the stairs behind me. Then he rushed at me and pushed me hard, throwing me off balance. I reeled backward, stumbled over a box on the floor, and started to fall. My hands scrabbled for something to grab onto but didn't connect with anything. I landed with a crash. My head snapped back and hit the floor. I felt something sharp against the side of my face, close to my ear. For a moment I lay dazed on the concrete floor.

Duffy stood over me, his coat pockets bulging, a can of peaches in each raised hand. I cringed, terrified that he was going to hurl the cans at me. But he didn't. Instead, he stepped over me and thumped up the wooden stairs to the kitchen.

My head hurt. I felt disoriented, but I forced myself to sit up. The side of my face burned. I had to grip the wooden banister with both hands to steady myself as I staggered up the stairs. By the time I got to the top, Mr. Duffy was gone. Ben bustled through the kitchen door carrying a coffeepot. He stopped when he saw me and gave me a peculiar look.

"What happened to you?" he said.

"Did you see Mr. Duffy?" I said.

"Mr. Duffy? Why?"

"I caught him in the basement, stealing food. When I tried to stop him, he attacked me." My legs were trembling. Duffy had really scared me. "Where's Mr. Donovan?" I said.

"I think he's in his office, but—"

I headed for the door.

"Whoa, wait," Ben said. He caught me by the arm. "You're bleeding."

"What?" My hand went to the right side of my face. When I pulled it away again there was blood on my fingers. I bent down and twisted my head to see my reflection on the side of the toaster on the counter. Blood was oozing out of what looked like a nasty gash on my face, close to my right ear. It had soaked into the collar of my sweater. I felt faint at the sight of it and reached for the counter as my knees began to wobble.

Ben was beside me in an instant. He gently tucked my hair behind my right ear and pressed a clean towel against the wound. He snagged a chair with his free hand. "Sit back," he said. He eased me down onto the chair. "Let me take a look." He pulled the towel away gingerly and then quickly pressed it back against my face. "I think you should get that looked at," he said. The somber expression on his face scared me.

"How bad is it?"

"Where's your coat? I'll get a cab. We'll go to the hospital. It isn't far."

"But Mr. Donovan—"

"First things first," Ben said. "Wait here."

When he came back a few moments later, he was wearing his jacket and carrying mine. He helped me into it, told me to keep applying pressure to the wound, and whisked me out the side door. When we got to the street, he flagged a cab. Andrew, the scruffy young guy who had recognized me by my boots, was standing near the curb when Ben helped me in and told the driver he wanted to go to the nearest emergency room.

"Hey Ben, is everything okay?" Andrew said as Ben climbed into the taxi beside me. Ben didn't answer. He slammed the door shut and asked the driver to hurry.

We waited for nearly a half hour in the emergency department of the closest hospital. Ben kept getting up and going to the main desk to tell them that I was bleeding. Finally, a nurse led us to a small room where we waited some more until a doctor appeared and examined me. Diagnosis: a mild concussion (he handed me a pamphlet on head injuries) and a facial laceration (why does *laceration* sound so much worse than *cut*?). "I'm going to put a couple of stitches in," the doctor said. The next thing I knew, he'd stuck a needle into my face. "Local anesthetic," he explained. "This may pinch a little."

.   .   .

"With any luck," the doctor said when he had finished, "there won't be a scar."

Scar?

"And if you don't wear your hair back," he said cheerily, "no one will notice."

Right after the doctor finished with me, someone knocked on the door. It was Art Donovan. He glanced at Ben before asking if I was all right. I said yeah, even though my head still hurt. All I could think about was the possibility that I'd end up with a scar on my face. After I told him what the doctor had done, he came closer and looked at the bandage.

"I called your father," he said. I had listed him as my emergency contact on the volunteer info sheet. My father tends to be a lot calmer than my mother in tough situations, probably because he used to be a cop. "He's on his way here."

"How did you know where we were?" Ben said.

"Andrew saw you and Robyn leaving the shelter in a taxi and heard you tell the driver that you wanted the nearest ER. He said he thought Robyn had been hurt." Art gave Ben a sharp look. "You've been with us long enough to know the procedure, Ben. When someone is injured, I'm to be notified immediately."

He turned to me. "Do you want to tell me what happened, Robyn?"

"It was an accident," Ben said. "When I saw she was bleeding, I panicked." I looked at him. He had seemed perfectly calm and levelheaded to me. "I decided I should get her to the hospital right away. I was going to call you."

"Wait outside, Ben. I'd like to talk to Robyn alone."

Ben's eyes caught mine and he stared hard at me, as if he were trying to tell me something. He nodded at Art and shook his head. What was that about? Then he went out into the hall. Art closed the door behind him and listened quietly while I told him what had happened. When I finished, he said, "Mr. Duffy can be a little unpredictable. I'm sorry. Do you want to press charges?"

"Press charges?" I hadn't even considered that. "I don't think he meant to push me as hard as he did." At least, I hoped he hadn't. "I guess after what happened yesterday, he doesn't like me very much."

"Yesterday?" Art said.

Uh-oh. Betty had told Ben not to mention Mr. Duffy's cookie-stealing episode to anyone.

"What happened yesterday, Robyn?"

Duffy had stolen food. At least twice. Surely Art had a right to know. I told him what had happened.

"Ben says he's harmless," I added. "But, to be honest, he scares me a little."

"For the most part, Ben's right," Art said. "Don't worry, Robyn. I'll have a talk with Mr. Duffy."

My father arrived. Art spoke briefly to him. He asked my dad the same thing he had asked me—whether he wanted to press charges. My dad looked at me. I shook my head.

"If this man was violent toward you, Robbie, he could be violent toward other people," my father said.

"He usually doesn't give us much trouble," Art said.

My dad looked skeptically at him before turning back to me.

"Mr. Donovan is going to talk to him," I said.

"I'm going to make myself very clear," Art assured my father.

My father still looked doubtful, but he said the choice was mine. Just before Art left, he said, "I hope this won't stop you from volunteering with us again, Robyn." My dad gave him a sharp look. After he left, dad inspected me.

"Your mom is going to be upset when she sees that," he said, taking a closer look at the dressing on my face.

Talk about an understatement. She was going to freak out. She was already overprotective, especially after what had happened with Nick. This was only going to make things worse.

"Actually, Dad, I was hoping I could stay with you tonight."

"Sorry, Robbie, no can do."

"What do you mean, 'no can do'?"

"You know I love it when you visit—"

"*Visit?* You told me when you and Mom split up that I would always be welcome at your place because it's my place too. My second home."

"My place *is* your place. But if I know your mother, she's already pacing up and down. She's going to want to see for herself that you're all right."

"You *told* her?"

"I called the hospital on the way over to see how you were," my father said. "Then I called your mom. I told her that there had been an incident at the homeless shelter and that you'd been taken to the hospital to get checked out, but there was nothing to worry about. The only reason she's not here right now is that I swore I'd call her as soon as I found out what was going on."

"But Dad—"

"And I promised to take you straight home. Give me a break, Robbie. If your mom found out that you'd had stitches and I hadn't told her, she'd skin me alive. Now come on." He helped me into my coat.

Ben was out in the hall. As he came toward me, he and my dad exchanged looks. Then my dad said, "I'm going to call your mother. I'll be right back."

"Nice going," Ben said after my father stepped outside with his cell phone. "Why didn't you just call the cops and have Mr. Duffy arrested? At least that way he'd have a nice, warm cell and a hot meal."

"What are you talking about?"

"I talked to Mr. Donovan," he said. "He's going to bar Mr. Duffy from the shelter for a week."

"I didn't ask him to do that," I said. "He asked me if I wanted to press charges, and I said no. But Mr. Duffy *was* stealing. And because of him I had to get stitches. Just because he's homeless, that doesn't mean—"

"How would *you* like to be out in the cold for a whole week?" Ben said. "How would you like to have no place to go?" Before I could answer, he wheeled around and walked away. What was with him? He had been so nice to me when he saw I was hurt, but suddenly he was acting like I had attacked Duffy instead of the other way around. Well, that was his problem. I went to look for my father.

.   .   .

My mother rushed out of the house as soon as my dad's car pulled into her driveway. She turned pale when she saw the bandage on my face and the information sheet on head injuries that my dad handed her.

"It's a *mild* concussion," my dad and I said in unison. "It sounds worse than it is," he added. "She's fine. Really." My mom glowered at him as though my injuries were his fault. She said, "You're not going back to that homeless shelter. Do you understand me, Robyn?"

I told her not to worry, that I had no intention of going back. I'd had all I could take of Mr. Duffy—and of Ben Logan.

And of Nick. I wouldn't have been anywhere near the shelter if it hadn't been for him. He still hadn't called. Where was he?

CHAPTER **FOUR**

That night the temperature plummeted. The forecast called for another few days of severe cold. Billy called me on Monday night.

"How are you feeling, Robyn?" he said. He'd asked me the same question a dozen times at school that day. He said he knew Mr. Duffy, but that he'd never known him to attack anyone before. He said he hoped I wasn't going to think that all homeless people did things like that, because it wasn't true.

"Still fine, Billy," I said. I had spent the whole day trying not to think about the possibility of a scar on my face.

"Mr. Donovan just called me," Billy said. "The city has issued a cold alert. When that happens, the shelter operates twenty-four hours a day instead of closing overnight. I was wondering . . ."

"Don't even think about asking, Billy," I said. I had promised myself on my way home from the hospital that I would never set foot in that homeless shelter again, no matter who asked me. Even if I'd wanted to go, my mother would never let me.

"They're really short on people, Robyn," Billy said. "Especially now. It's hard enough to get volunteers at night, especially on short notice. It's even worse so close to Christmas. Nothing will happen, I promise. We'll be working in groups. I'll make sure you're safe. Please? I wouldn't ask if it wasn't important."

Now that I had actually been to the shelter, it was much easier to picture how much the place meant to the people who relied on it and so much harder to tell myself that it wasn't my problem. Still . . .

"I don't know, Billy . . ."

"They need people to help inside, and they need people in the vans."

"Vans?"

"They do patrols. They round up anyone who's sleeping outside, bring them in out of the cold. You would be in one of the vans with me. Come on, Robyn. It's brutal out there. This is the kind of night when people could literally freeze to death."

I pictured Andrew. I pictured the women with the bundle buggies who had been clustered around the TV.

"Well . . ."

"I'll meet you at the bus. We'll go together."

I hesitated.

"What about Morgan? Is she coming too?" I said.

"She can't. She's got some family thing."

Family thing? She hadn't mentioned any family thing to me.

"So you'll come, right?" Billy said.

"Well . . ." If it were anyone else, I would have said no. But it was Billy, and Billy was so kindhearted that he was making me feel like a grinch.

"I'll talk to my mom," I said. "I'll call you back."

My mother started shaking her head before I'd even finished explaining what I wanted to do.

"I thought we agreed you weren't going back there," she said.

"But Billy says they're shorthanded."

"That may be, but after what happened the last time you were there—"

"I don't think that man meant to hurt me, Mom. Besides, he's been barred from the shelter. And anyway, I'm not going alone. Billy's going to be with me."

My mother started to relent. She comes across like a mother lion when it comes to making sure I'm safe, but she isn't hard-hearted. And, like everyone else, she liked, trusted, and respected Billy.

"Billy said we might be late," I warned her.

"Robyn, it's a school night."

"I know. But I have a spare first thing in the morning. And it's not like we're doing much. Most teachers are giving us class time to finish projects and essays, and all of mine are done." Come Friday morning, we would be off school for a two-week winter break. "It's for a good cause. It's cold tonight. All I'm going to do is help people stay warm."

"What about you?" she said. "How are *you* going to stay warm? And how will you get home?"

"I'll be in a van," I said. When she still didn't look convinced, I added, "I'll bundle up. Promise. And when I'm finished, I'll hop a bus over to Dad's place. It's not that far from the shelter." My father lived downtown. My mother lived uptown in a more suburban neighborhood.

Eventually, after double-checking that I had packed extra mittens and making me promise that I would keep my hat on my head, my mom let me go.

.   .   .

Art Donovan came over and welcomed me when I arrived with Billy.

"This means a lot to us, Robyn," he said. "You can't believe how busy we get on a night like this."

I looked around and was surprised to see how many people were already bedding down on foam mattresses and fold-up cots.

"The regulars know that when it gets this cold, we'll be open for the night, so they show up on their own," Art said. "But there are a lot of other people out there who don't know or who need coaxing. We find them, tell them the shelter is open, and bring them back here—if they want to come. We have a lot of territory to cover.

I've assigned both of you to Eileen. Billy will introduce you—I think Eileen's in the kitchen—and fill you in on what you'll be doing. Okay, Billy?"

Billy had explained everything on our way to the shelter. Some people, he said, prefer to sleep outside—no matter what. They can't tolerate the cramped quarters of an emergency shelter or they're afraid someone will steal their few belongings. We would try to persuade everyone to come back to the shelter, but we couldn't force them. Anyone who insisted on staying outside would be given hot soup and an extra sleeping bag to get them through the night. Billy also told me that there was a team assigned to each of the shelter's two vans—a professional social worker with enough medical training to know when a person either had to come in out of the cold or be transported to a hospital, and two volunteers whose job it was to hand out the soup, warm clothes, and sleeping bags. We headed for the kitchen.

As soon as Billy pushed open the kitchen door, I spotted Ben. He was loading cartons of soup into insulated boxes. Betty worked alongside him. Another volunteer was packing boxes of foil-wrapped sandwiches. Ben looked up when we entered the room and greeted Billy warmly. He didn't say anything to me, and I didn't speak to him either. Billy asked Betty where Eileen was. She nodded to the kitchen's rear door. We went out into the parking lot behind the church and found a thin, serious-looking young woman wearing a big hat with earflaps and the thickest pair of mittens I had ever seen.

She was piling sleeping bags into the back of a van. Billy introduced me and asked her what she needed us to do. She sent us back into the kitchen for soup, which we loaded into the van.

"I think that's everything," Eileen said ten minutes later, her words turning into frosty swirls in the frigid night air. "Let's get rolling."

We had been assigned the west side of downtown. Eileen and Billy knew exactly where to look. We found people huddled under mounds of blankets and dirty sleeping bags, on top of subway vents, in bus shelters, in the entrances to stores and office buildings. Every time we spotted someone, Eileen stopped the van, got out, and asked the person if he or she wanted a ride back to the shelter. Mostly they were men, but there were a few women, some couples, and even two people with dogs.

If the person didn't want to leave his or her spot, Eileen made a note of where we had found the person and promised everyone who chose to stay on the street that someone would be back later that night to check on them. If people wanted to get in out of the cold, Eileen brought them back to the van and then drove to the next spot on our route. When the van was full, we drove back to the shelter.

Billy and I waited in the foyer while Eileen showed the passengers inside and helped to get them settled. A second van pulled up and Ben got out. He made no move to speak to me, which suited me fine. When Eileen came out of the shelter, we set off again.

The next three people we found refused a lift back to the shelter. Eileen tried to coax them. She warned them how cold it was going to get and what could happen to them if they stayed outside. When she had exhausted all of her arguments, she summoned me, and we made sure that each person had something warm to eat and a clean, new sleeping bag to keep them warm. By midnight we had given out almost everything we had and had transported more than fifteen people back to the shelter.

"I'd like to make one more run before we call it a night," Eileen said. "Everyone okay with that?"

Billy and I nodded. I called my dad and let him know what was going on.

"You're going to be tired tomorrow, Robbie," he said. "Let me know when you're done, and I'll come and get you."

We did one more circuit, each of us looking for the lumps of blankets and sleeping bags that marked another homeless person. For a long time, we saw no one.

"Up there," Eileen said, pointing to a bus shelter ahead of us.

"Over there," Billy said at almost exactly the same time, pointing to a figure lying in the doorway of an office building. Eileen stopped the van.

"I'll check the bus shelter," Eileen said. "You two go and check out that doorway."

Billy waited for me to join him, and we set off across the street to investigate the blanketed figure.

The person—I couldn't tell if it was a man or a woman—lay on top of a couple of old sleeping bags, covered only with a thin, worn blanket. On a night as cold as this, I wondered, why wouldn't the person have used the sleeping bags to cover up? I shivered as a gust of arctic air sent some old newspapers swirling. An empty bottle, propelled by the wind, rolled out of the alley next to the building and stopped at my feet. I glanced at it—a whiskey bottle.

"We'd better wake him up," Billy said. "It's the only way to make sure he's okay." He started to bend down.

"Wait!" I said, grabbing his arm.

So far everyone we had approached had been awake or had at least stirred at our arrival. But this person seemed to be fast asleep. What if Billy startled him—or her? What if the person responded by attacking him? My mind flashed back to my encounter with Mr. Duffy in the homeless shelter basement.

"I have to wake him up, Robyn," Billy said. "It'll be okay. I've done this before."

I stood back a few steps, just to be on the safe side, and watched him bend down and reach for a shoulder. He gave a gentle shake.

"Hello," he said. "Hello."

No response.

I edged in close to Billy. The person hadn't moved. Billy pulled the blanket down a little so that he could see who he was shaking. It was a man with a scruffy beard. He was lying on his side with his face pressed in against the door. Billy shook him again, more vigorously this time. The man fell over onto his back—Mr. Duffy. But his eyes were still closed.

Billy glanced at me. Then he shook him again, even harder.

"Mr. Duffy," he said. "Wake up, Mr. Duffy. We've got a hot drink for you."

There was something funny about the way he was lying. So still. Too still. I crouched down beside Billy, no longer afraid that Duffy would lash out at me, and loosened the scarf, stiff with grease and grit, that was wound around his neck. Billy looked bleakly at me as I pulled my mitten off and gingerly pressed my fingers against his neck to check for a pulse.

"You'd better get Eileen," I said.

. . .

Eileen did the same thing I had done—she felt for a pulse. Then she fished out a cell phone, called 911, and asked them to send an ambulance.

"Is he—" Billy began.

"I'm not a doctor," Eileen said, her face grim. "So I have to call. It's procedure."

Eileen urged us to go back to the van to wait, but I couldn't make myself go. I kept checking my watch, waiting for the paramedics to show. Maybe it wasn't hopeless. Maybe there was something they could do.

Finally the paramedics arrived. So did a police cruiser. After the paramedics had examined Mr. Duffy and contacted a hospital, Duffy was pronounced dead. The police called the coroner. Billy turned and walked back to the van. He sat there, his head bowed slightly, until the police approached him. They talked to each one of us alone. They asked me to tell them everything I knew about Mr. Duffy. It didn't amount to much. They asked me twice exactly when we had spotted him, what we had done when we approached him, what we had touched, and where exactly we had stepped.

"What happens now?" I heard Billy ask one of the police officers.

"The coroner will probably order an autopsy," the officer said, "to determine cause of death." He gave us a sympathetic look as he closed his notebook. "What you kids are doing is great. If there were more people like you around, the world would be a better place."

By the time the police left, it was nearly two in the morning. On our way back to the shelter, I got out my phone and called my dad again.

"Robbie, I was just about to call you," he said. "I was getting worried." When I told him what had happened, he said, "You and Billy stay put. I'll be there as soon as I can."

When we got back to the shelter, everyone seemed to know what had happened. Eileen and Art Donovan huddled together in the outside the front door. I saw Billy talking to Ben. Ben glanced at me, a grim expression on his face. My stomach clenched when he and Billy walked toward me.

"I still can't believe it," Billy said. "Mr. Duffy was practically the first person I met when I started volunteering here. I saw him almost every time I came down."

Ben looked sharply at me. "If you hadn't said anything to Mr. Donovan, Mr. Duffy wouldn't have been barred from the shelter. He would have showed up on his own when the temperature dropped. We wouldn't have had to go looking for him. And you wouldn't have found him dead."

I stared at him, stung. Was he right? Was I responsible?

"Hey," Billy said. "It's not Robyn's fault. We don't even know how he died. Maybe it's like the police said. Maybe it was natural causes. Or something else wrong with him. You know as well as I do that people on the street develop all kinds of health problems."

I sure hoped that Billy was right.

"Sure," Ben said. "It's the coldest night of the year and we find him dead under one thin blanket. Definitely natural causes."

"He could have gone someplace else," I said. "There are plenty of shelters—"

"He didn't feel comfortable in most of those places," Ben said. "But he felt safe here. I told Mr. Donovan that."

That was news to me.

A sleek, black Porsche pulled up outside. I raised a hand to wave at the driver. Ben arched an eyebrow as he looked from the car to me. I felt his eyes on me, but I refused to look at him. I grabbed Billy's hand, and we ran down the steps and got into my father's car.

CHAPTER **FIVE**

The next day, when Morgan and I were on our way out of school, she nudged me in the ribs.

"Look who's here," she said, grinning at me. She pointed down the stairs. Ben was leaning against the wall just inside the main doors. "He's really cute, Robyn. You two would look great together."

"He hates me, Morgan. He practically accused me of killing a homeless person."

"I know. But that's ridiculous," she said. "He probably came to apologize." She waved at him. "Hi Ben."

Ben nodded in acknowledgement, but he kept his eyes on me. Morgan poked me with her elbow again.

"If I end up with a bruise, you're going to be sorry, Morgan."

"Look at the way he's looking at you," she whispered. "He's definitely interested. I can tell." She flashed me another grin, said, "I have to run," and retreated to a bank of lockers down the hall, where she pretended to busy herself with a lock that wasn't hers.

Ben stood where he was. He stared at me but didn't say a word.

"What's the matter?" I said. The way he was looking at me gave me the creeps.

"Mr. Duffy didn't die of natural causes. It wasn't a heart attack or a stroke or anything like that."

If you'd just glanced at him, you would have thought he was perfectly calm. You had to look closely to see that he was trembling all over. I started to get a bad feeling.

"What did he die of?" I said, even though I was pretty sure I already knew the answer.

"He froze to death."

I felt sick inside.

"That's awful," I said. "I'm sorry."

"You should be." He was blaming me. He was definitely blaming me.

"I'm sure everyone who knew him is sorry, Ben."

"Right," he said. "But it's not *everyone's* fault. If you hadn't ratted him out to Mr. Donovan—"

"I'm sorry," I said again. "But I was upset. He scared me. I was bleeding." I touched the ugly bandage on the right side of my face. "I told Mr. Donovan that I didn't think he meant to hurt me. I never meant for anything to happen to him."

"I wish you'd never come down to the shelter," Ben said. "Then this never would have happened."

"I'm sorry," I said. "I'm really sorry."

Ben glared at me a moment longer before turning and stalking out of the school.

Morgan came back to join me. "I guess that didn't go so well, huh?" she said.

．　·　．

"Do you think I did the wrong thing?" I asked my father when I got to his place after school.

He looked surprised.

"Why?" he said. "Do *you*?"

"Well, he *was* homeless," I said.

"That's hardly your fault, Robbie."

"But if I hadn't told Mr. Donovan what happened—"

"I know how you must feel," my father said. "It's a real tragedy that he froze to death. It's a tragedy that anyone freezes to death in this day and age, especially in a big city like this. But it sounds to me like he had problems besides being homeless."

"I know," I said. Still, I couldn't stop thinking about what Ben had said. "But if he hadn't been barred from the shelter, he might still be alive."

"If he hadn't become aggressive with you, he probably would have become aggressive with someone else. If it had been another volunteer in the kitchen when he snuck down into the basement, even if it had been a staff member, he probably would have acted the same way. You're lucky you weren't badly hurt, Robbie."

"If it had been someone else, they might have handled it better than I did."

My father looked at me for a few moments. "I could think of a hundred ifs, Robbie," he said. "But it is what it is. All you did was answer Mr. Donovan's questions truthfully. After that, it was out of your hands. You had no way of knowing what he was going to do. And you certainly had no way of knowing that this man would sleep outside on the coldest night of the year instead of making his way to an emergency shelter. As I understand it, he had been homeless for quite some time. He must have known there were other places to go."

I knew my father was trying to make me feel better. I even knew that most of what he was saying was true. But it didn't help.

.   .   .

"It's terrible that that old guy froze to death," Morgan said when I called her later. "But it's not exactly a first. It happens every year."

"I know. But everyone thinks it's my fault."

"*Everyone?*"

"Well, Ben does. And I wouldn't be surprised if Billy did too."

There was silence on the other end of the phone.

"He does, doesn't he, Morgan?"

"Billy's a nonjudgmental person, Robyn."

That was true. "But there's no way he would ever rat on a homeless person," I said.

"Come on, Robyn, you know Billy. He would probably have given the guy every cent he had to go and buy food if he thought he was hungry enough to steal. But for what it's worth, if it had been me? I would have pressed charges."

I love Morgan. She's my best friend. But somehow what she said didn't make me feel better.

"I gotta go," I said. "I have to call Billy. I need Ben's phone number."

. . .

When Ben agreed to meet me, he was about as enthusiastic as a person booking an appointment for major dental surgery. When I sat down opposite him that night in a coffee shop he'd chosen, he gave me a sour look.

"It was on the news," he said. "Did you see it?" I hadn't. "Homeless man freezes to death. First one this winter." He sounded angry. "Do you know how many homeless people froze to death *last* winter?" I didn't. "Four. The winter before that it was three. But nobody cares."

"I wouldn't say that—"

"You know what the worst part is? The worst part is that no one even knows who he is—who he was."

"What do you mean?"

"All anyone knows about Mr. Duffy is his name. No one's even positive that Duffy *was* his real name."

"Come on," I said. "People must know more than that. Someone must know where he came from. He must have had some identification."

Ben shook his head. "Mr. Donovan said the police couldn't find any. All he had on him when he died was a couple of paperback novels and a wad of paper napkins. The police asked around, but no one knows anything about him. They don't know where he came from or how he ended up on the street. Even his first name. Mr. Donovan says they fingerprinted him at the morgue to see if they could identify him that way. But they couldn't. He won't even get a real headstone. He'll end up getting a cheap funeral at city expense. But what's the point, huh? They wouldn't even know what name to put on the grave. He'll just be one more pathetic, anonymous homeless guy who drank too much and froze to death."

"Drank too much?"

"He'd been drinking. They think he passed out and that's why he froze to death."

"Oh," I said. I thought about the whiskey bottle I had seen on the sidewalk near where we had found Mr. Duffy.

Ben's eyes zeroed right in on me. "What does that mean—'Oh'?"

"Nothing," I said quickly.

"I know what you're thinking," Ben said. "When people see homeless guys like Mr. Duffy having a drink or smoking, they think they're committing some kind of crime. They think if homeless people didn't smoke or drink, they'd be able to afford food or a place to stay. It doesn't work that way. They're on the street because they're sick or because they've hit bottom and they can't get back up again. Sometimes a smoke or a drink is the only pleasure they have in life. It's not a crime. And, anyway, Mr. Duffy was trying to quit. Mr. Donovan told me."

Too bad he hadn't succeeded, I thought.

Ben shook his head impatiently. "When I heard you were Billy's friend, I thought maybe I'd been wrong about you. But I guess I wasn't. You don't see someone like Mr. Duffy as a real person—someone who deserves the same things in life that you have."

"That's not true," I said. "I called you because I feel terrible about what happened and because I want to know if there's anything I can do. Anything at all."

"Right," he said.

"I mean it, Ben."

"Really?" he said. "Anything?"

. . .

I arrived back at my dad's loft just in time to see his (young) friend Tara leave the building and climb into a taxi. I wondered how she figured into my father's life. The whole time my parents were separated, he acted as if he thought they would eventually get back together. They never did. He had seemed stunned when my mother finally divorced him. But as far as I knew, he hadn't yet become seriously involved with another woman. My mother, on the other hand, was seeing Ted Gold—Ted had even proposed to her. My mom hadn't said yes, but she hadn't said no, either, and it seemed to me that she and Ted were closer than ever. Had my dad finally decided to move on?

I found him sitting on a stool in his kitchen, sipping coffee and reading the newspaper. He glanced up when I came through the door.

"Robbie," he said. "Where did you disappear to?"

"I had to meet someone."

"I've got something for you," he said. He slid off his stool, went into the living room, and picked up some papers that were lying on the coffee table. He handed them to me.

I scanned the top page. *Autopsy report*, it said. *Last name: Duffy. First name: Unknown. DOB: Unknown. Age: Approximately 60–65.*

"Where did you get this, Dad?"

"From the pathologist. She faxed this over to me—at my request."

"She?"

My father grinned and took the report from me. "Basically what it says is that your Mr. Duffy was in poor health." He ran a finger down the page. "At some point in the past, he suffered a serious head trauma, which may at least partly explain why he was on the street. He also suffered damage to his face. Serena says he must have had poor vision in his left eye."

"Serena?"

"The pathologist. And—the big one, Robbie—the man ingested a *lot* of alcohol just before he died."

"I already know that, Dad."

"You do?"

"Ben told me."

"Maybe someone treated him to some pre-Christmas cheer. Or maybe he collected enough change to buy himself a bottle. Some people think that alcohol will warm them up on a cold night. They don't realize the risks it poses."

"Is that supposed to make me feel better? Because it's having the opposite effect."

"What I'm saying is, if he drank as much as Serena says he did, then he probably passed out. And that could just as easily have happened even if he hadn't been barred from the shelter. You drink that much, Robbie, and you don't think straight. You did tell me that he was lying *on top* of a couple of sleeping bags, didn't you? He wasn't in them or covered by them. That suggests to me that he passed out before he could take even the most basic precautions against the cold. It's not your fault, Robbie. Chances are what happened would have happened no matter what."

Maybe he was right. But I still couldn't shake the feeling that Ben had a point. If I hadn't said anything to Art Donovan, the night might have turned out differently for Mr. Duffy. He might still be alive.

"Nobody knows anything about him, Dad. According to Ben, no one even knows if Duffy was his real name. They don't know what happened to him, if he had any family. Ben says he's going to be buried at city expense."

"At least he gets a funeral and a burial," my father said.

"But no full name to go with it. Ben says that Mr. Duffy didn't have any identification on him—no birth certificate, no driver's license, no passport. No old letters or bills. Not even a library card. How can that be, Dad? Everyone has some kind of ID."

My father shrugged. "Maybe he lost whatever he had. Maybe it got stolen. Or maybe he stashed any valuables he had in a safe place so they wouldn't get stolen."

"The thing is, Ben wants to do something for Mr. Duffy," I said. "He doesn't want him to be just one more anonymous homeless person who froze to death. He wants to find out more about him so that he can hold a memorial service." Ben had been so earnest when he'd told me what he wanted to do. He had also been sure that I wouldn't care. But I did. Okay, so maybe guilt had a lot to do with why I'd offered to help. But the more I thought about it, the more it seemed like the right thing.

My father arched an eyebrow. "You seem to care an awful lot about what this Ben thinks."

"It's not about Ben. It's about Mr. Duffy. I want to do something. But I don't know where to start. The police tried to identify him by his fingerprints, but they struck out."

"All that means is that the man didn't have a criminal record."

Mr. Duffy had been so aggressive with me that I found it difficult to believe he'd never been in trouble with the law.

"What about dental records?" I said. "Can't they use those?"

"Dental records are only useful if you have some idea who the person is," my father said. "Otherwise, how do you know which of the hundreds of dentists in the city to check with? And that's assuming Duffy was originally from here or that he had dental work done while he lived here—which, based on Serena's report, seems doubtful."

"But someone must have some kind of record of him, right?"

"Not necessarily."

"Great. So basically I volunteered for Mission: Impossible."

"Why do you say that?"

"Because if the police can't find out—"

"The man froze to death, Robbie. As far as the police are concerned, his death was an accident. They did what they could to find out who he was, but it's not a high priority if no crime was committed. Mission: Impossible, though? I wouldn't jump to that conclusion."

"You mean there's a way we can find out who he was?"

"I wouldn't necessarily say that, either."

"Then what *would* you say?"

"If it were me, Robbie—if someone hired me to find out who he was—you know what I'd do?"

I shook my head.

"I'd talk to people."

"But Ben said—"

"The man lived in this city. He interacted with people. He was a regular at the homeless shelter, probably at other shelters or soup kitchens around town, too."

"But if no one at Mr. Donovan's shelter knows anything about him—"

"Oh?" my father said. "You spoke to all the staff and all the regulars there?"

"Well, no, but—"

"One person might know one little thing. Another person might know something else."

"So I should talk to people at the shelter?"

"It would be a start. You could also check out Duffy's turf."

"His turf?"

"Beggars usually stake out a spot that they consider their own. They're there day after day. And there are bound to be people who pass that same spot every day, maybe on their way to and from work. Some of them may have dropped money into Duffy's hat. Some people make a habit of it—a quarter or two every day."

"You think that some of them might have talked to Mr. Duffy?"

"It's worth a shot. Just because Mr. Duffy didn't have a regular place to stay doesn't mean he wasn't in contact with people. For example, he had to get his clothes from somewhere."

"Maybe from secondhand stores," I said.

My father grinned. "And I doubt he spent all his spare time at the shelter," he said. "If he was begging, then he probably had some cash at least some of the time. He probably spent it on food or drink, maybe on toiletries."

I thought about checking with some of the stores and restaurants in the area. This was beginning to sound like a big job.

"Did he have anything on him when they found him?" my dad said. "He carry anything with him? Some homeless people drag their belongings around in a bag or a cart."

I thought back to the night we had found Mr. Duffy. "All I saw were those sleeping bags and that old blanket," I said. "I don't remember any bags or a cart. Ben said that Mr. Donovan told him that all Mr. Duffy had with him were a couple of paperback novels and some paper napkins."

"What about a liquor bottle?"

"There was a bottle rolling around near him."

"You remember what it was?"

"Sure. That Napoleon stuff you and Vern like to drink."

"Cognac?" my father said. He sounded surprised. "Doesn't sound like something a homeless person would be able to afford. But I guess you never know."

"Maybe that wasn't his bottle."

"You're probably right," my father said. "Those books, though, they could be interesting."

"You mean I could check out where he got them?"

"Or if there's anything tucked inside."

"What about those napkins?" I said. "Maybe they have a restaurant logo on them."

My father looked positively proud of me. "Good thinking, Robbie. Also, where did he hang out when he wasn't at the shelter? In a park? A library?"

"Or a parking garage. Billy says lots of homeless people sneak into garages to get warm."

"Is there a walk-in clinic in the area?"

"I can check." But I was definitely going to need help. "Thanks, Dad."

He grinned. "Hey, I like puzzles. That's what this is. A gigantic puzzle. But before you can begin to solve it, you have to hunt for the pieces." His face grew more serious.

"What?" I said. "Is something wrong?"

He hesitated.

"I ran into Ed Jarvis today," he said finally. Ed Jarvis had been Nick's probation officer.

My heart started to race. "Does he know where Nick is? Is he okay?"

"He didn't even know that Nick was gone."

"So he hasn't talked to him? He has no idea where he is?"

It looked like my dad was going to say something, but he hesitated again.

"What?" I said. "What'd he say?"

"Only that it's possible that Nick got into trouble again and that's why he took off. He says he's seen it happen before—kids straighten out for a while and then they mess up. When they do, they sometimes go out of their way to avoid the people who have helped them. They're ashamed of slipping and they're afraid they've disappointed the people who care for them."

"You don't think Nick—"

"I don't know what to think, Robbie. I'm just telling you what Ed said, and he knows Nick a lot better than I do."

I struggled to keep back my tears. I missed Nick. I wished I knew where he was. But I didn't, and until he contacted me there was nothing I could do.

CHAPTER **SIX**

"I hate this," Morgan said at eleven thirty the next day. We had a double lunch period followed by PE, which had morphed into library time because our PE teacher was out sick. Morgan had been ecstatic when she'd heard. She'd wanted to spend the extra time doing Christmas shopping. Instead I had convinced her to come down to the shelter with me so that she could help me talk to people. I had asked Billy too—the more, the easier?—but he had a review lab he couldn't miss.

"How can you hate it?" I said. "We haven't even started."

In fact, we had just got off the bus. Morgan was clutching a giant latte, which she had insisted she needed to "keep her going."

"I mean, I hate that it's so dirty and depressing down here," she said, shivering inside her faux-fur coat as she glanced up and down the street.

It had snowed about a week ago, which had made some neighborhoods, like my mother's, look like a scene from a Christmas card—snow-covered lawns; white pine trees; all that snow reflecting the glow of Christmas lights. But not this neighborhood. In this neighborhood a layer of grime and litter had settled on the once-pristine snow. Not a festive sight.

"I bet you don't complain when you're down here with Billy," I said.

She shook her head. "If I did, Billy would take it as a criticism of homeless people." She sighed. "He's so sweet. I adore him, really I do. He doesn't think poor people can be held responsible if their neighborhoods are dirty and depressing. But come on, it doesn't cost anything to pick up after yourself. Am I right?" She gulped down the last mouthful of her latte and looked around for a garbage can. There were none in sight. "Huh," she said. She held onto the cardboard coffee container, if only to prove her point. "So, now what?"

"Now we start talking to people. We might as well begin in the obvious place." I nodded down the street toward the shelter. A knot of smokers had gathered in a circle outside the main door. Morgan looked apprehensively at them.

"What if they won't talk to us?"

"If they won't, they won't."

"What if some of them are, you know . . ." I waited, pretending I didn't know. "You know," she said again. "A little . . . crazy?"

"You've spent more time here than I have, Morgan. Why are you acting like you're afraid of these people?"

"You're telling me you're not?"

"They're homeless. They're not criminals."

"Then why did you beg me to come with you? Why didn't you come down here alone? Or if this is so important to Ben, why isn't he here instead? It would give you two a chance to become better acquainted. Billy says he's nice when you get to know him. And he's really hot, Robyn."

"First of all, I offered to do this. Me. Not him. Second, I'm *not* interested in him."

"But with Nick gone—"

"I don't want to talk about Nick. I just want to do what I said I'd do. I asked you to come with me because you're my best friend. We have to talk to *a lot* of people. Two people can cover twice as much territory."

"Right." Morgan did not sound convinced. She trailed half a step behind me as we walked the rest of the way to the shelter. When we got there, the smokers ignored us.

"Excuse me," I said.

They continued to ignore us. I moved closer to the small circle and tapped one of the smokers on the arm.

"Excuse me, sir."

He turned. So did everyone else. He was about my height, with stubble all over his chin and a cap with earflaps pulled down low on his forehead. He glowered at me from beneath the visor. His mismatched eyes—the left one was dark, the right one cloudy white—made him look particularly sinister. He was smoking what looked like a hand-rolled cigarette, held with cold-reddened fingers that poked out from the unraveling ends of woolen gloves.

"Hi," I said again, trying not to stare at the milky eye. "I was wondering if I could ask you—all of you—a few questions about Mr. Duffy."

It was already cold outside, but it suddenly got a lot colder. Half of the smokers shifted their eyes to the ground. A couple shuffled away down the sidewalk. A couple of others, including the man with the mismatched eyes, stared hard at me. I wondered if they knew that I had ratted on Duffy. Morgan tugged on my elbow, but I held my ground.

"I'm helping Ben," I said. "You know Ben?" Nothing. Not a nod, not a glint of acknowledgement in anyone's eye, certainly not a friendly smile. "Ben wants to hold a memorial service for Mr. Duffy. He asked me to help him by talking to people who knew Mr. Duffy. So he can say something about Mr. Duffy at the service."

The two men who had been looking at me looked away. The men who hadn't already left moved down the street, away from the shelter and the two uptown girls who were asking questions.

"Well, we're off to a good start," Morgan said, watching them. "What do you say we go inside, where we can at least be warm while we're being ignored?"

It was the first good idea Morgan had had all morning.

"Why don't we talk to whoever's in charge around here?" Morgan said. She glanced around the interior of the drop-in center, spotted a garbage can, and rid herself of her giant latte cup. "I bet they know something."

Art Donovan spotted me and came over to us. "Ben told me what you're doing," he said. "I wish I could help. But Mr. Duffy never said much to me. In fact, he seemed to go out of his way to avoid talking to me."

"You must have some kind of records, some kind of information on him," Morgan said. "Ben said he was here all the time."

Art smiled pleasantly at her. "It's Megan, isn't it?" he said, which surprised me. He struck me as someone who was good with names.

"Actually, it's Morgan," Morgan said.

"Morgan," Art said, as if he were trying out the name. "Sorry. You're right about Mr. Duffy being here a lot. But I'm afraid we don't have any records. Not on Mr. Duffy, anyway. Or most of the people who use the shelter, for that matter. Our mandate is to offer a safe place for the homeless to get out of the cold—or, in summer, out of the heat—provide them with something to eat, and help them get whatever services they might need. Anything they may require and will agree to."

"Did Mr. Duffy use any services?" I said.

"Not that I know of. He was pretty independent. He never made any trouble, either." When I looked skeptical, he said, "Well, up until about six months ago. Mostly, Mr. Duffy was quiet and kept to himself. It's only recently that he started acting up. Maybe he said something to Betty. She chased him out of the kitchen often enough."

"Who's Betty?" Morgan asked after Mr. Donovan had left.

I sighed. It was just like Morgan to volunteer somewhere and not remember the names of staff.

"She's the cook," I said.

"Great. Let's go and talk to her." She grabbed my hand and started to drag me across the room.

"The kitchen's *that* way," I said, pointing in the opposite direction.

When we got to the kitchen door, Morgan nudged me in ahead of her. "This is your project," she said. "You ask."

I sighed and led the way inside.

"What do I know about Mr. Duffy?" Betty said after I had told her why we were there. She thought for a moment and shrugged. "Not much, I'm afraid. Except that he liked my beef and barley soup. He always asked for seconds."

"He never told you anything about his life?"

"Not a thing."

"Did you ever ask?" Morgan said, sounding exasperated, as if it were Betty's job to at least know *something*.

"Well, I didn't pry, if that's what you mean," Betty said a little stiffly. "A lot of the people who come here don't want to talk about their past lives. It's too painful for them to think about the times when things were better. Or, for some of them, when they were worse. Some people end up on the street because of tragedy or misfortune—they get sick or they lose their jobs or families. Other people run to the street because it's better than whatever they used to call home. So a lot of them don't appreciate being quizzed about their personal lives any more than anyone else does. If they tell me something, fine. But I don't go around asking. And Mr. Duffy—well, he never volunteered anything."

"What about the food he stole?" Morgan said.

I blushed. I didn't want Betty to think that I'd been badmouthing Mr. Duffy. But Betty just shook her head.

"He particularly liked to stock up on cookies," she said. Then she frowned. "He never used to be one for desserts. He must have developed a sweet tooth."

I thanked her for her time.

"This will go faster if we split up," I told Morgan. "I'll talk to the people eating breakfast. You talk to the people who are watching TV." She looked at the half dozen camped out around the television. She didn't move. "They're just people," I said, trying to convince myself as much as her. What if they looked at me the way Ben did—like I was a two-four who dropped by once and then vanished? What if one was like Mr. Duffy? But we were already there, and I had made a promise. "Some of them, if not most, knew Mr. Duffy. I bet they'll want to help us."

Morgan looked doubtful. We split up, and then regrouped twenty minutes later.

"Well, that was fun," Morgan said, clearly disgruntled. "How did you make out?"

"Not great," I said. "Except for that man at the end of the table, no one would even talk to me." I nodded to an old man who was two overcoats and glistening with sweat as a result. "But he didn't want to talk about Mr. Duffy. He wanted to talk about how someone took his stuff last winter." He had told me he always wore all his clothes at the same time so no one could steal them. "What about you? Did you find out anything?"

Morgan shook her head. "Nobody knows anything—not his first name or where he came from or how he ended up on the street. Or if they *do* know, they're not telling. If Ben's relying on my information, pretty much all he'll be able to say is that Mr. Duffy quit drinking for good before he died."

"Quit drinking? What are you talking about?"

She gave me an exasperated look.

"Am I speaking Swahili or something? Someone told me that Mr. Duffy quit drinking for good a few months ago."

"Morgan, he died because he passed out after drinking too much."

"I'm *aware* of that," Morgan said. "I'm just telling you what a woman told me. She said that he'd quit drinking. She thinks the police are lying about how he died—that they're saying he was drinking because they're trying to blame *him*, when the real reason he died is that he was barred—" She broke off suddenly. "Sorry," she muttered. "That's what she said. I—"

"Who told you that, Morgan?"

"The woman in front of the TV." She turned to point. "Oh," she said, deflating a little. "She was there a minute ago."

"What was her name?"

"I didn't ask. Look, Robyn, I'm sure she just—"

"It sounds like she might have known Mr. Duffy pretty well," I said. "Maybe she knows something more. What did she look like?"

"Like a bag lady? Middle-aged. She was wearing a *lot* of clothes. And she had a little buggy parked beside her chair."

"You mean Aggie," said a voice behind me. I turned toward it.

"It's Andrew, right?" I said.

He seemed pleased that I knew his name. He peered at the bandage that was half hidden by my hair. "Are you okay?"

"I had to get a couple of stitches," I said. "But I'm fine." Still, I started fingering the bandage and wondering again about a possible scar.

"I heard you asking about Mr. Duffy," he said. He had a funny, mumbly way of talking. His lips hardly moved, and he kept his head bowed a little so that, even though he was taller than me, he seemed to be looking up at me while he spoke.

"Do you know anything about him, Andrew?"

He shook his head. "He never talked to me. He didn't talk much to anyone. I seen him with Aggie a couple of times, though."

"Do you know where we can find her?"

He shook his head again. "But she'll be back. She always comes back."

"Do you know where Mr. Duffy spent his time when he wasn't here?"

"He liked an office building over on Victoria Street," Andrew said. "It was his place. He did pretty good there too, considering how he treated people."

"What do you mean?" Morgan said.

"He yelled at them sometimes."

I knew what he meant. I remembered how Mr. Duffy had cursed at the man who had dropped a five-dollar bill into his hat.

"I seen him do it a couple of days ago," Andrew said, looking shyly at Morgan. "A man was trying to give him something—"

"Money?" I said.

"I don't know. I guess. He was holding something out to Mr. Duffy, and Mr. Duffy was yelling at him. He was all huddled over, you know, like maybe he just wanted the man to go away. It was weird, but Mr. Duffy is like that sometimes. If some guy was trying to give me money—if *anyone* was trying to give *me* money—you know I'd take it."

"Where was this?" I asked.

"Same place," he said. "In front of the office building." He peered at me. "Why are you asking so many questions about him?"

"Ben wants to hold a memorial service for him. I'm trying to help," I said.

He thought about that for a moment. "If I hear anything," he said, "I'll let you know."

I watched him make his way to the door and wondered what had brought him to the street.

Morgan and I were on our way out of the shelter when Art Donovan called my name.

"I have something for you," he said. He handed me a photograph. It was a group shot of what looked liked clients of the homeless shelter. "That's Mr. Duffy," he said, pointing to the man on the far left. "It's not the greatest picture in the world, but it's the only one I could find of him. You can have it if you want."

"Okay, that's that," Morgan said cheerfully once we were out on the street again. "Let's go shopping."

"Not yet."

"Aww, come on, Robyn. There are only nine more shopping days left."

"You said you'd help me, Morgan."

"Excuse me, but what was I just doing?"

I gave her a look.

"Okay, okay," she grumbled. "What do you want me to do?"

CHAPTER **SEVEN**

"**N**ow can we go home?" Morgan said a few hours later. "My feet are killing me. I'm cold. And I still have spit on the front of my coat. That stuff sticks like glue. What if that woman—"

"Aggie. Her name is Aggie."

"Right. What if *Aggie* has a communicable disease?"

"Why are you acting so squeamish today? You volunteer at the shelter."

Morgan's cheeks, already red from the cold, got a little redder.

"You *do* volunteer there, don't you, Morgan?"

"I'd like to," she said. "I know it's important to Billy. But you know how unpredictable my schedule can be."

"So exactly how many times *have* you been down here?" I said.

"Come on, Robyn. If I came down here every single time Billy asked me to, I'd never have any time for myself."

"How many times?"

"I was here once at the beginning of November."

"For how long?"

"What difference does it make?"

"For how long, Morgan?"

She shrugged and looked down at the sidewalk. "Couple of hours."

"A couple of *hours*?"

"I had a hair appointment. I dropped by to pick up Billy when I was finished, and I helped him sort out some clothing donations."

"And since then?"

"Well . . ."

That explained why Art Donovan hadn't remembered her name. I should have known. Morgan was my best friend. She was madly in love with Billy, even though she and he were polar opposites. But she was *not* a people person, especially not a homeless-people person.

"I thought volunteering to help live people would be better than volunteering to pick up dead birds," she said. During the last migration season, Morgan had spent a day sorting through dead birds collected by the Downtown Avian Rescue Club. She had spent the following week complaining about the stench of death that she claimed clung to her hair. "It turns out I was wrong."

"Sooner or later, Billy is going to expect you to actually show up," I said.

"Maybe by then he'll be involved in something else. You know, something I can handle."

Uh-huh.

"Robyn, can we *please* go somewhere warm?"

I looked up and down the street. The only possibility I saw was a place called Sal's Open Kitchen. It looked decidedly down-market. I glanced skeptically at Morgan.

A gust of icy wind caught us both, and we shivered.

"I can hardly feel my fingers," she said. "And my face feels numb. I could be drooling and not even know it. If Sal's is heated, that's good enough for me." She changed her mind as soon as she pushed open the door. "On second thought, maybe we should go someplace else."

"The closest someplace else is at least five blocks that way," I said, pointing.

"But that's *into* the wind," Morgan said. She took another look at Sal's long, narrow interior. One side was taken up by a counter that ran the length of the place. Three of its stools were occupied. Half a dozen four-person tables filled the other half of the room. A couple tables at the rear were occupied by men drinking beer.

"Maybe if we sit up front," Morgan murmured. She headed for the table closest to the window and gingerly inspected a scarred, vinyl-covered chair before dropping down on it.

. . .

"I still can't believe she spat at me," she said. Morgan had spotted Aggie, the woman she had talked to at the shelter, as we were dividing up the places that we needed to visit.

"I guess she doesn't like to be called a liar," I said.

"Well I guess *not*," Morgan said. "But why did she spit at *me*? You're the one who made her angry."

Morgan had dragged me over to where Aggie was standing, rooting through some garbage bins in an alley alongside a convenience store, and had demanded, as only Morgan can, that Aggie repeat what she'd said earlier about Mr. Duffy. At first Aggie didn't want to talk, so Morgan fished in her pocket and surrendered all of her spare change. Then, when Aggie repeated what she had told Morgan, Morgan looked triumphantly at me. When I (stupidly) told Aggie what everyone else had said—that Mr. Duffy couldn't have quit, because he had passed out from drinking too much—Aggie had flown into a rage. That's when she'd spat at Morgan.

"I think she was aiming at me," I said, "if it's any consolation."

"It isn't," Morgan said.

A sad-looking man in a grease-spattered apron shuffled over to us.

"I'll have a latte," Morgan said.

The man shook his head and gestured at the menu signs that hung over the counter.

"I think your choices are coffee, tea, or beer," I said.

She looked at me as if I must have been mistaken.

"Espresso?" she said to the man.

He shook his head again.

"Two coffees," I said.

The man shuffled away.

"Perfect," Morgan muttered.

"Let's drink our coffee, get warm, and go over what we found out. Then we'll get out of here," I said. My dad had been right. When you start out knowing next to nothing about a person, when that person doesn't have any forms of ID, it takes a lot of legwork just to gather some puzzle pieces, never mind assembling the puzzle. "I'll go first."

"No, *I'll* go first," Morgan said. "I want to get this stuff out of my head and out of my life."

The aproned man slid a couple cups of murky coffee in front of us. Next to each cup were two little containers of cream. Morgan peered at them as if they contained poison. But she peeled the tops off both of them, sniffed the contents, dumped them into her cup, and stirred. She took a sip and made a face.

"Well, at least it's hot," I said.

Morgan made a face, pushed her coffee aside, and started to tell me what she had found out: "He hung around at least three of the six thrift shops in walking distance of the homeless shelter. I say *at least* 'cause the people I talked to at the other three shops couldn't say for sure whether he'd ever been in their stores. That photo that Mr. Donovan gave us isn't the greatest." We had made a photocopy of it. Morgan had taken the original with her. I'd shown the copy to a few people, but Mr. Duffy's face was pretty hard to make out. "But for sure Mr. Duffy visited three places on and off over the years, looking for a pair of pants, a shirt, a sweater—stuff for winter. But—and explain this—lately he started looking for other stuff: clothes for a small girl, a warm coat for a woman. When he bought that stuff, he always ended up bringing it back a couple of days later. *Always*. What do you think that's all about?"

I had no idea.

Morgan continued: "There are two pharmacies in the area and two small grocery stores. The people in all of those places recognized Mr. Duffy. They all acted like I was crazy when I asked about him. They said he was a nuisance. One of the pharmacies got a clerk to follow him around whenever he was in the store. They were sure he was stealing stuff. But they never actually caught him. The man who owns one of the grocery stores said the same thing—except he actually caught Mr. Duffy in the act. The man said he was taking packages of spices—coriander, cumin, stuff like that." She looked intently at me, checking to see if I grasped what she was saying. "Fruit, bread, canned goods—that would make sense. But why would a homeless guy steal spices? The man said Mr. Duffy begged him to let him keep the stuff. The guy finally gave in, but he told Mr. Duffy that he'd call the police if he ever came back. He said Mr. Duffy was so grateful that he actually thanked him.

"I went to the public library. Sometimes people like Mr. Duffy go there to beat the weather. The librarian I talked to was really nice. She remembered him and said mostly he was well behaved. She said there are several homeless people who stop by regularly. They just want a place to sit for a while. She said that Mr. Duffy read a lot of magazines. Especially computer magazines. Like, cover to cover. And you know the couple of shelves of old books that have been taken out of circulation, that they sell for a fifty cents or a dollar? She said Duffy bought one or two almost every time he came in. Novels, usually classics—Dickens, Tolstoy. Lately, though, guess what? He started buying picture books. Kids' books.

"He visited the neighborhood walk-in clinic every couple of months." When she saw my expression change, she added, "Yeah, I perked up when I heard that too. I thought maybe we'd lucked into something. But no one could tell me anything about his medical history, *of course*. That's confidential. Apparently he always insisted on seeing the same doctor. Turns out *he's* out of the country with Doctors Without Borders. I left a message on his office phone in case he ever calls to check his messages. Who knows? Maybe he'll get in touch with you. And that's it—that's all I could get."

I stared at her.

"What?" she said, annoyed—at me, at the spit on her coat, at the lukewarm non-latte coffee, at our surroundings.

"You did good, Morgan."

"You sound surprised."

I *was*, a little. I had asked Morgan to help me, and she had agreed. But deep down I'd had my doubts about her ability (or willingness) to coax information out of complete strangers about another complete stranger.

She leaned back in her chair and crossed her arms over her chest. "So," she said, "what did *you* find out?"

What I had found out, item one: "I talked to workers at the two shelters around here. They both said more or less the same thing. They know him only by the name Duffy. They have no idea where he came from, what his past life was. No idea how he ended up on the street."

"Are you detecting a pattern here, Robyn?" Morgan said.

I continued: "One of the workers I talked to has been at the shelter for maybe five years. He said that Duffy used to sleep at the shelter from time to time, but not very often. Both of them said that he didn't feel comfortable at the shelters." Ben had told me the same thing.

"But you hear yourself, right, Robyn? Mr. Duffy did know where those shelters were. He could have gone to one if he'd wanted. He didn't *have* to sleep outside."

Maybe.

"They also said that in the past few months they'd caught him sneaking in a couple of times and stealing stuff. They never pressed charges. They just made him leave. And both of them said that up until recently, Mr. Duffy drank *a lot*. They said most of the money he made begging probably went to buying booze."

Morgan reached for her coffee cup, and for a moment I thought the caffeine addict in her was going to win out over the quality-snob. But she sighed and tucked her hands in her lap.

Item two: "Mr. Duffy was a regular at the soup kitchen at St. Brigit's Church. They offer a hot meal there at noon every Tuesday and Thursday. He showed up at least once a week. Never talked to anyone. He never caused any trouble, either—until recently, when he started filling his pockets with extra food, which is strictly against the rules. They let you take a sandwich and a piece of fruit for later in the day, but that's it. Mr. Duffy started taking more."

Item three: "I described Mr. Duffy and showed his picture around in ten, maybe eleven, coffee shops and fast-food places in the area where he asked for change. Only two people recognized him, and one of them wasn't one hundred percent sure. They both said he came in from time to time, bought a coffee, and then sat at a table until they had to ask him to leave. Only one person, a guy who works at a place called the Black Cat Café, knew Mr. Duffy's name. *That* guy said he let Mr. Duffy use the phone a few times—which he wasn't supposed to do—including a couple of days ago. But he doesn't know who Mr. Duffy called."

Item four: "There are dozens of underground parking garages in the area." They were all cold and horrible and scary. But I had trudged down to the tollbooth in each of them and showed the picture that Mr. Donovan had given us. "They all said the same thing, Morgan. They always find homeless people—usually more than one—sleeping somewhere inside when the weather is cold. Usually in stairwells, if they can get in. And usually they let them stay, at least until about seven the next morning, when the commuters start to arrive. But nobody remembered Mr. Duffy specifically."

"Great," Morgan said. "So we froze our butts off all day and, basically, we don't know any more about Mr. Duffy than we did when we started."

"We know a few things," I said.

"But not his first name. We don't know anything about his past life. We don't know why he's homeless. We don't even know where he's from." She stood up. "Let's get out of here."

I glanced at my watch. "We got down here far too late to catch people on their way into work."

"So?"

"So, people will be heading home soon. Mr. Duffy begged in the same location every day. Maybe some people gave money to him regularly. Maybe some of them know something about him."

Morgan shook her head. "No way," she said.

"No way what?"

"You want to stand out in the street accosting people, don't you?"

"Well, I—"

"How are you even going to get them to stop?"

Good question. "Maybe if we—"

"We?" Morgan said. "You're my best friend, Robyn. I'd do anything for you—up to a point. But my feet are sore, I have a headache, I have dried spit all over my coat, and I promised Billy I'd meet him at"—she consulted her watch—"right about now. I gotta run. Come on, Robyn, let's call it a day."

"You go," I said. My feet were sore too. I also had a headache. I didn't have spit on my coat, but I *was* discouraged. Still—"I'm going to stick around."

Morgan glanced at the men at the tables around us. "I don't think this is the best place for a girl alone—"

"I don't mean here," I said. "I'm going to try to talk to people who might have given Mr. Duffy money. I'll have to do it sooner or later. I might as well get it over with." I dug out some money and slapped it onto the table to pay for our coffees.

We went outside. It was colder now than it had been earlier, or maybe it only seemed that way after we'd been inside for a while.

"Robyn, are you sure?"

I nodded. How hard could it be, right?

CHAPTER **EIGHT**

How do you convince tired, busy people hurrying through a cold, dark evening to their cars or to catch a bus so they can get home to their families or dogs or cats to stop and chat? Once they've stopped, how do you find out what they know about a scarred, cantankerous old homeless man who recently froze to death?

I stood near the corner outside the medium-sized office building where Mr. Duffy had asked for change on weekdays. It was the same building where I had seen him the first day I went to Art Donovan's shelter. In another thirty minutes, people would start to pour out of the building—and all of the surrounding buildings. Some of them must have paused at least once to throw money into Duffy's hat. Why else would he have come back to the same spot every day? But how would I get any of them to stop? If I approached one person, I would miss five or ten others—maybe people who knew something—while I explained what I was doing to that one person, who might know nothing at all. I thought for a few moments and then headed across the street.

.   .   .

By the time I got back to the spot where Mr. Duffy used to beg, there were only two thoughts on my mind: 1) *I hope this works*, and 2) *I'm really glad that Morgan can't see me now*.

Then: "Robyn?"

I whirled around. "Ben? What are you doing here?"

He stared incredulously at me. When he finished reading the front of the homemade sandwich-board sign that I was wearing, he circled around to read the back. "Do you think that's going to work?" Ben asked.

I shrugged. "It would probably be better if I had someone to help me."

He smiled. It amazed me how that simple change of expression could transform a person's face.

"What do you want me to do?" he said.

What Ben did was draw attention to me and my signs. Some people shook their heads as if they thought I might be crazy. Some smiled, also as if they thought I might be crazy. A few people came up to me and said that they'd heard what had happened, but that they hadn't known that the man who froze to death was the same man they walked past every day. A lot of people said that they had dropped money into his hat every now and then. Almost all of them said how sad it was that in such a big city, there were so many people who had no roof over their heads. My brilliant plan wasn't exactly an overwhelming success. A grand total of four people said they had actually exchanged words with Mr. Duffy.

"I used to buy him tea on the really cold days," an older woman said. "I can't remember how I found out that he liked tea, but he did. The first time I offered him a cup, I was nervous. I thought he might be insulted. But he wasn't. He thanked me so politely. But that's all I know about him."

"I heard about that man," said another of them, a man with an expensive-looking briefcase. "That was him, huh?" He shook his head. He really seemed to care. "I wish I knew more about him," he said. "Mostly he didn't say much. I remember one time, though, after I'd been on vacation, he mentioned he hadn't seen me around. He asked me if I'd been sick. That really surprised me. When I told him I'd been out west, he said he bet the daffodils were out on the coast already. I remember being surprised at that too, because I hadn't given much thought to where he might have come from. You don't, do you, when you see someone asking for change? So I asked him if that was where he was from."

I held my breath.

"He didn't answer," the man said.

I tried to hide my disappointment.

"He'd had a head injury," I said. "Maybe he couldn't remember."

The man shook his head. "If it wasn't for bad luck, I guess he'd have no luck at all, huh?" Before he left, he asked me for the name of the homeless shelter and said he'd make a donation.

"I tell you what," the third person, another man, said. "He knew something about computers. I had dropped some money into his hat—every day at the end of the day I drop all my spare change into some homeless person's hat. Why not? Who wants to drag around a pocketful of coins? Anyway, a week or so ago, I'd dropped all of my change into his hat and I was talking to a buddy of mine, a software developer, like me. Just chit-chatting. My buddy mentioned this project he was working on had him stumped, and the old guy—what did you say his name was? Duffy?—he gave my buddy a suggestion. While he was talking, the lights came on in my buddy's eyes. That old guy knew what he was talking about. Turned out it was a good suggestion. Just the other day my buddy asked me if I'd seen the guy around. He wanted to talk to him. You say he's the guy who froze to death, huh? Terrible way to go." He dug out his wallet and pressed a wad of twenties into my hand. "You give that to that shelter of yours," he said. "It's not much, but . . ." He shrugged.

And, finally, from a grandmotherly woman: "I heard about what happened. What a shame. That little girl is going to miss him."

"Little girl?" I glanced at Ben. He looked as surprised as I was. "What little girl?"

"There was a little girl who used to come by and talk to him," the woman said. "My office is right across the street." She pointed to an elegant stone building across the street. "He used to smile when he saw her coming. I think it's the only time I ever saw him smile."

"Do you know who she is?" I said.

The woman shook her head. "She looks about five or six years old. She always comes by with her mother. At least, I assume it's her mother. They're South Asian—Indian or Sri Lankan, I'm not sure."

"Do you know if they came regularly? Maybe at a particular time or on a particular day?"

The woman shook her head again. "I didn't pay that much attention. I just used to look out the window sometimes and see the girl and her mother. The little girl would be talking to the man you're asking about."

"Do you know when they were here last?"

"I'm sorry," she said. "I really don't know anything else."

As she walked away, an elegantly dressed man came up to me and said he'd been listening to what I'd been saying. He thought what I was doing was "admirable."

"It's always so gratifying to see a young person take such an active interest in the community," he said.

"Did you know the man who used to sit around out here?" I said.

"To be honest," he said. "I'm not sure. I've been tossing coins into several hats every day. It will probably sound terrible to you, considering what you're trying to do here, but I don't pay a lot of attention. I see whatever they're using to collect money, and I throw something in."

I'd thought Mr. Duffy had a face that was impossible to forget. But when I described him, the man shrugged apologetically.

"I'm in town for the next couple of weeks. My company is setting up a new office right up there," the man said, pointing. "If it will help, I'll ask around the building and see if anyone there knows anything."

"I'd appreciate it." I hunted around for a piece of paper, scribbled down my name and number, and handed it to him. "This is where you can reach me," I said.

"Robyn," he said, reading what I had written. "I'll remember that. How did you come to know this man?"

"I didn't really know him," I admitted. "But my friend Ben did." I waved Ben over and introduced him. "Ben volunteers at the shelter that Mr. Duffy liked to go to."

The man chatted with Ben for a few moments about the shelter. Then he pulled out a business card and wrote something on the back.

"Here's a number where you can reach me," he said. "I'd be interested in knowing if you ever solve this little mystery of yours."

I tucked the card in my pocket.

"Nice guy," Ben said.

"All the people who stopped to talk were nice," I said. The four who had taken a few moments to try to talk to Mr. Duffy made me feel a little ashamed. The most I had ever done was drop a few quarters into a hat.

The rush-hour crowd had thinned. I shivered uncontrollably as I pulled off my sandwich-board sign.

"I guess that expensive jacket isn't as warm as it looks, huh?" Ben said.

"For your information, I've been out all day talking to people—"

"I'm just teasing," he said. For once he didn't seem to be angry with me or to be making fun of me. "Come on," he said. "Let's go someplace where you can warm up."

He steered me to a cozy, delightfully warm restaurant. We claimed a booth near the back and shucked our coats and hats. Ben dropped his backpack onto the floor beside him. After a waiter handed us menus, I glanced at Ben.

"What are you doing down here anyway?" I said. "Are you checking up on me?"

"Actually, yes," Ben said.

That made me angry. "I told you I'd do whatever I could to find out about Mr. Duffy. Didn't you believe me?"

"Of course I did," he said.

"But you still came to check up on me?"

"I came to make sure you were all right. And to see if I could help."

"How did you even know I was here?" I asked.

He smiled at me. "Billy's girlfriend called me."

"Morgan?"

He nodded. "She told me what you were doing. She suggested that I come down here." He laughed. "Actually, more than suggested. She said she thought it was totally unfair that you were freezing your butt off down here while I was lounging around in a nice, warm house."

That sounded like Morgan. I bet I knew why she'd made the call too, and it wasn't just because she thought I needed a hand. She thought Ben would be the perfect replacement for Nick. But I wasn't interested in a replacement.

"She's right," Ben said. "I shouldn't leave it all to you. I've been thinking about what I said the other day. I was mad. I hate that Mr. Duffy died the way he did. But I shouldn't have taken out my frustration on you."

We ordered. While we waited for our food, I said, "Well, at least we know a little more about him now than we did before."

"We do?"

"Sure. You heard what some of the people out there said. I'd bet that Mr. Duffy spent some time out west. We know he liked tea. We know that he knew enough about computers to impress someone who's in the computer business."

"He liked to surf the Internet at the shelter sometimes," Ben said. "I asked him one time what kind of sites he liked to visit, but he didn't answer."

"Well, he may not have talked much, but he wasn't completely antisocial, either. Sounds like that little girl made him smile." I thought about that for a moment. "The librarian Morgan talked to said he bought used paperbacks from the library."

"I know," Ben said.

"You do?"

"The two books he had with him? They were from the library. They were stamped *Withdrawn*."

"Morgan said that up until recently he bought grown-up books," I told Ben. "Then about six months ago, he started buying kids' books. Maybe they were for that little girl. He also bought children's clothes at a secondhand store. But he always brought them back for a refund." I hadn't figured that one out. "How long did you know Mr. Duffy, Ben?"

"Almost a year. I started volunteering at the shelter last January. It was my New Year's resolution—do something good for someone else."

"What was he like when you first met him?"

"What do you mean?"

"Morgan and I talked to a lot of people today. From what everyone said, it seems that something changed in Mr. Duffy's life about six months ago." I went over everything that Morgan and I had found out. "Till then he was drinking. But he stopped. Until six months ago, he didn't cause trouble at any of the shelters or soup kitchens he visited. Then he started taking things—food, mostly. All of a sudden he was buying children's clothes."

"Which he returned," Ben said.

I nodded. "Up until about six months ago, no one at any of the stores he went in ever complained about him. Then he started stealing. He stole spices from a grocery store." I asked Ben the same question Morgan had asked me. "Why would a homeless man with no access to a kitchen steal spices?"

"Maybe he gave them to Betty," Ben said.

"We talked to Betty. She would have mentioned it." It was so frustrating to have uncovered such tantalizing little bits and pieces but to be no closer to the truth. "I have no idea what it all adds up to," I said.

The waiter returned with our food. I couldn't believe how hungry I was. I plunged into my grilled chicken salad.

"Do you think maybe we should just leave it alone?" Ben said. "Drop the idea of a memorial service? You know, respect his privacy?"

"I don't know. Maybe." What to do about the memorial service was Ben's decision. I was thinking about what the woman said about the little girl and her mother. And about the spices Mr. Duffy had stolen. I wondered if the woman and the little girl knew that Mr. Duffy had died. "What happened to the books Duffy had with him?"

"I have them right here," Ben said. He picked his backpack up off the floor. I stared at it.

"What's that?" I said.

"What's what?"

"That." I pointed to the crest on his backpack. I hadn't noticed it before. "Does that say Ashdale Academy?"

Ben's cheeks turned pink.

"How come you have a backpack with an Ashdale crest on it? Do you go there?"

Ashdale Academy was a private boys' school uptown. I'd heard called the most expensive, most exclusive boys' school in the city. Ben looked at the few remaining French fries on his plate. He straightened up slowly and nodded.

"Uh-huh," I said, digesting this new fact. "So where exactly did you get off giving me a hard time because of how *I* dress and the car *my* dad drives?"

"Would it help if I apologized?"

"It would help if you explained."

He drew in a deep breath "The first time I saw you, I thought I knew you," he said. "I mean, I thought I knew your type. Like the girls who live in my neighborhood. The girls who go to St. Mildred's." St. Mildred's was the most exclusive private *girls'* school in the city. "Most of them have no idea what real life is like. Their idea of struggle is waiting a week until the Prada bag they ordered comes in."

"You think I'm like *that*?"

"Thought," he said. "Past tense. I was wrong. I'm sorry." He looked at me, and for a moment I looked back. Then I thought about Nick.

"Right," I said. "Let's see those books." I held out my hand.

"I don't think they're going to tell us anything." Ben fished the beat-up novels out of his Ashdale backpack.

Ours hands touched as Ben passed the books to me, and our eyes met again. I looked away quickly and told myself that I didn't want to get involved with anyone else, even if he turned out to be a whole lot nicer than I had originally thought. I told myself that Nick was the one for me—Nick, who had left town without a word to anyone. A wave of anger washed over me. I blocked both Ben and Nick out of my mind and turned my attention to the two books.

CHAPTER **NINE**

Both of the battered paperbacks that had been in Mr. Duffy's pockets when he died were written by Charles Dickens. One was *Great Expectations*. The other was *Hard Times*. I flipped through them. A business card was tucked in the pages of the first book—from one of the best hotels in the city. I held it up so Ben could see it.

"He must have picked it up somewhere," Ben said. "Probably used it as a bookmark."

I held the front and back covers of each book and shook them gently. A slip of paper fell out of *Hard Times*. I picked it up and looked at it.

"Anything useful?" Ben said.

"It's a receipt." I studied the faint ink. "From a thrift store." In fact, it was from one of the shops that Morgan had visited earlier that morning. "But I can't tell what he bought—it only says 'clothing' and the price. And the date. About two months ago."

"In other words, not useful," Ben said.

I turned the receipt over. Someone had written what appeared to be a phone number on the other side, followed by the letter *F*.

"Would you recognize Mr. Duffy's handwriting if you saw it?" I said.

Ben shook his head. I looked at the phone number again. It had been written in pencil and had faded, but it was still legible. The numbers were formed in a thin, elegant hand.

"Doesn't look like a man's handwriting," I said. "And it sure doesn't look like the handwriting you'd expect from a homeless person."

"A homeless person who likes tea and Charles Dickens and daffodils?" Ben said.

He had a point. I had thought of Mr. Duffy as just a crazy old man who stole cookies and shoved people when he got mad, a man who was nothing besides what you saw. But he had come from somewhere. And he must have started out like everyone else: young and with the potential to become almost anything. It was possible that he had spent his whole life on the street, but it didn't seem likely. There just had to be a way to find out more about him. I looked down at the faded receipt. Then I dug into my bag, pulled out my cell phone, and started to punch in numbers.

"Who are you calling?" Ben said.

A phone rang somewhere at the other end of the line. It rang again and again until someone finally picked up.

"Hello?" A man's voice.

"Hello," I said. "Who am I talking to?"

"Who do you *want* to talk to?" the man said. He sounded annoyed.

"Is Morgan there?"

Ben gave me a funny look. "Morgan is at Billy's house," he said.

Instead of telling me that I had the wrong number, the man at the other end of the line called out, "Is there a Morgan here?" The number on the back of the receipt didn't belong to a private residence. I must have called some kind of public place. The man came back on the line. "You're out of luck," he said. "There's no one here named Morgan."

"Um, where is here, exactly?" I said.

"Look, sweetheart, you made the call. I just picked up the phone. Your friend isn't here, and a dryer just opened up. If I don't grab it, someone else will and I'll have to go home with wet undies, you know what I'm saying?"

Dryer? Wet undies?

"Morgan left me a message," I said. "She wanted me to bring her some fabric softener, but she didn't give me the name of the place or the address."

I heard the man shout, "Touch that dryer and you die!"

"Hello? Hello?"

He told me the name of the coin laundry and the main intersection. Then he hung up.

"What was that all about?" Ben said.

"The phone number on the back of this receipt—I think it's a pay phone at a laundromat a couple of blocks from the shelter."

"The place where Mr. Duffy washed his clothes."

"I guess." I started to hand him back the books, but Ben shook his head.

"Every time I look at those books, I feel terrible. I know Mr. Duffy didn't have much—but to think that a couple of secondhand books were his only possessions . . . I hate to throw them out, but . . ."

"If you want, I'll hang onto them for you. Just let me know if you want 'em back."

Ben nodded, and I stuffed the books into my bag.

"Come on," Ben said. "I'll walk you to the bus."

I fished out my wallet, but Ben waved it away.

"Dinner's on me," he said. "After everything you've done, I feel I owe you one." On the way out of the restaurant he said, "By the way, the funeral is the day after tomorrow."

"The day after tomorrow? But we don't know—"

"It is when it is. The way things are going, we won't be able to say much about him, and it looks like there will never be a complete name to put on the headstone."

"Headstone?" I knew the city would pay for the funeral and the burial. But a headstone? "Aren't those expensive?"

"I'm going to pay for it—well, with a lot of help from my father." There was no warmth in his words. "At first he said it was a waste of money." He looked fiercely at me. "He was going to buy me a car for Christmas. I told him I wanted this instead. Maybe no one can say much about Mr. Duffy at his funeral, but if we ever find out his real name, he's going to have a headstone."

"I wish I could have done more," I said.

He shook his head. "I gave you an impossible mission, Robyn. But you did great. Really."

. . .

I almost fell over when my mother gave me permission to go to the funeral. I had braced myself for an argument.

"My heart isn't made of stone," she said when she saw my surprise. "That man's death is a tragedy. And, anyway, I doubt there's going to be much serious work done at school this morning."

There were a lot more people in the church than I had expected. Art Donovan was up front with Ben. So were Betty and a few other volunteers. I recognized some of the shelter clients too. And in the middle of the church, twisted around in her seat and watching the door, was Morgan, sitting next to Billy. She waved when she saw me. I gestured to her from the back of the church. She said something to Billy, who turned and smiled at me. Then she scooted out of the pew and came to meet me.

"We saved you a place," she said.

"I want to sit in the back."

"But Ben's up front. Don't you—"

"If I sit in the back, I'll be able to see everyone who comes in," I said.

"Are you expecting someone?"

"I'm not sure. Maybe."

"I'll go and get Billy," she said.

I shook my head. "You guys might as well stay put. I'll catch up with you afterward."

Morgan returned to her place next to Billy. I checked out the pews at the rear of the church. The last one on the right was empty, and there was only one person sitting in the one on the left—Andrew. He started to smile when he saw me and then quickly hid his mouth with his hand.

"What are you doing way back here?" I said, sliding into the pew beside him.

He shrugged shyly. "I like to be near the exit. You know. Just in case."

In case of what? I wondered.

"What about you?" he said. "Don't you want to sit with your friends?"

"I want to see who comes and goes."

"You mean you're staking out the place?"

"Sort of. I'm kind of hoping that a woman who knew Mr. Duffy will show up."

Just as the service started, someone slipped into the same pew as me and Andrew. A man in a long overcoat.

He had a black knit stocking cap pulled down over his eyebrows, and he didn't remove it. He looked at Andrew and me before turning his attention to the front. From the look of him, I guessed he was also client of the shelter. I wondered how well he had known Mr. Duffy, if. Duffy had ever spoken to him.

I continued to scan the crowd during the first half of the service. At one point Art Donovan got up and said a few words about Mr. Duffy. Mostly he said how quiet Mr. Duffy had been. Then Ben stood up and faced everyone. He glanced at a sheet of paper in his hand.

"I didn't know Mr. Duffy well," he said. "Nobody did. Like Mr. Donovan said, he kept mostly to himself." He looked out at the people scattered among the pews. Then he looked back down at the piece of paper. After a moment he crumpled it, drew in a deep breath, and said, "And that was his right—not to talk about himself, about who he was or where he came from. But I can't help thinking that it's too bad we don't know more about Mr. Duffy, because if we did, maybe people would care more about what happened to him. What could just as easily happen to other people like him. Most of the time, people don't think about them. If people hear that a homeless man died, that makes one kind of picture in their minds. But if they hear that a man who loved flowers and little children died, a man who liked to drink tea and read novels by Charles Dickens, that makes a whole different picture. Mr. Duffy froze to death in the middle of a big, wealthy city in a big, wealthy country. He froze to death because he didn't have a home to call his own. But because nobody knows anything about him, they don't get angry about it. And if we don't get good and angry about the fact that some of our neighbors don't have a roof over their heads, then how are things ever going to change? How are we going to make sure that something like this never happens again?"

He stopped abruptly and looked at Mr. Donovan. "I'm sorry," he said. "But that's how I feel."

There was dead silence in the church. Then Andrew started to clap, quietly and slowly. Someone in front of us joined in. Then someone else and someone else, until finally everyone was clapping. Ben was still standing at the front of the church. His face turned red. He said something to the minister and then went back to his seat. The minister waited until everyone had quieted down before speaking. "I don't believe I have ever heard applause at a funeral service," he said, "but I must say, I think the sentiment expressed by the previous speaker deserves the reaction that it received. In Luke, chapter three, verse eleven, John the Baptist says, 'Let the man who has two coats give one to the man who has none.' I think what our young friend was expressing . . ."

I didn't pay attention to the rest of what the minister said because I was watching a woman walk up one side of the church. She wore a thin coat and had a scarf over her head. Under the coat she had on brown and gold pajama-like pants and a matching tunic. She was carrying a small, plastic-wrapped bunch of flowers. She held a little girl by the hand. The woman hesitated when she reached the front of the church. She looked at the people in the pews. Then she pulled herself straight and led the little girl to Duffy's casket. She laid the flowers on top of it. Head bowed, she led the little girl back the way they had come.

"Andrew, do me a favor?" I whispered. "If I'm not back before the service ends, tell Morgan—my friend up there—that I'll call her. Okay?"

Andrew nodded. He didn't ask where I was going.

I got up and hurried out the church door. By the time I got outside, the woman and the little girl were scurrying down the street. I ran after them. Maybe they weren't the two people that had been seen with Mr. Duffy, but they sure fit the description.

Both the woman and the little girl looked impossibly underdressed for the cold. Both of them were wearing cheap sneakers instead of warm boots and thin, stretchy dollar-store gloves. Their thin coats that might have protected them from rain, but they must have been all but useless in keeping out the frigid December air. I caught up with them while they were waiting for a light to turn.

"Excuse me," I said.

The woman's dark eyes looked enormous in her thin face. She gathered the little girl against her and stared at me. She was shivering.

"I'm sorry to bother you," I said, "but I saw you at the church."

She just stared at me.

"I wanted to talk to you about Mr. Duffy."

"Duffy?" she said.

"You were just at the church," I said. "At his funeral."

The little girl looked up at her mother and said something in a small voice that I couldn't understand. The woman scooped her up and held her tightly.

"Someone told me that they'd seen you and your daughter talking to Mr. Duffy on the street," I said. I smiled at the little girl and she burrowed her face in her mother's scarf.

"Someone talked to you about me?" the woman said, her eyes widening in alarm. "Someone was watching me?" My father would have placed her accent immediately. He had a good ear—he loved to surprise people by pinpointing their place of origin based on a few sentences. But I was hopeless at it.

"No, no," I said. "No one was watching you. It's just that I've been trying to find people who knew Mr. Duffy, and someone said that they'd seen a woman and a little girl talking to him. So I was wondering—"

The woman's eyes shifted from me to somewhere over my shoulder.

"I'm sorry," she said. She looked nervous all of a sudden. "I must go."

Behind me, a voice said something in a language I didn't understand. I turned and saw an angry-looking man who was as underdressed for the cold as the woman and the little girl. His light jacket had a company name and logo sewn onto it. He scowled at me as he took the girl from the woman's arms. He said something else to the woman. She shook her head as she answered. As he started to walk away, carrying the little girl, the woman looked apologetically at me. Then she hurried after him.

"Wait!" I called. "If I could just ask you a few questions . . ."

The man turned and glared at me. He quickened his pace. I didn't know what to do. The woman seemed nervous. It was clear that this person, who I could only assume was her husband, didn't want her talking to me.

I watched them disappear around a corner. Then, as if I'd been tethered to them, I started to follow them. By the time I got to the corner, they were at the top of the next street. They turned again. I sped up, but when I reached the corner where they'd made their second turn, they had vanished. I stared up the street. There were at least thirty or forty houses on each side. They could have gone into any one of them.

Discouraged, I headed back to the church. On the way I noticed something I hadn't seen when I was following the family—a laundromat. The same one I had called after finding the phone number that had been tucked inside one of Mr. Duffy's books.

CHAPTER TEN

My phone trilled—again.

"Yes?" I said wearily.

It was Morgan. "Explain to me one more time why I'm freezing my butt off out here in the cold *again* instead of finishing my Christmas shopping at a nice, warm mall," she said. "You know, every time I volunteer to help you or Billy, I end up numb."

Morgan hadn't been my first choice for a helper. I had approached Billy, thinking that he'd sign on—and he would have, if he weren't already scheduled to be at the Humane Society. Morgan hadn't actually volunteered either. She had *wanted* to go home and soak in a nice, hot bubble bath. As she put it, "That church was hot and some of those people smelled bad to begin with and it only got worse when in the heat—no offense to them." Instead, I had talked her into coming back downtown.

I sighed. "Are you going to call me every two minutes to complain?" I said, glad that we weren't communicating face-to-face.

"We've been out here nearly an hour, Robyn. The sun is going down. It's getting *really* cold."

"If he's going to show, he's going to show soon," I said.

"How do you know he'll show at all?"

That question again.

"Because he was wearing a Night Owl Cleaners jacket," I said, *again*. "Night Owl cleans office buildings." I had been at my mother's office many times after hours when the Night Owl cleaners were there. According to my mom, the company had practically cornered the market on the downtown office towers. "They start as soon as everyone else has gone home, around five thirty or six. If he works for Night Owl, he's going to have to leave home soon or he'll be late."

"*If* he actually works for Night Owl," Morgan said grumpily.

"He was *wearing* a Night Owl jacket."

"Jason Ransome wears army fatigues to school, but he's not a soldier," Morgan said. "He gets them at a surplus store. He thinks they look cool."

I checked my watch. "If we don't see him by six o'clock, we'll leave," I said. "I'll even buy you a latte."

"And biscotti," Morgan said.

"Done," I said. If there was one thing I had learned during my long friendship with Morgan, it was that bribery definitely worked.

I had figured it this way: I knew which street the woman and the little girl lived on, but I didn't know which house. So I'd enlisted Morgan to stand at one end of the street while I stood at the other, watching to see which house the man came out of. After he was gone, we could go and talk to the woman. Maybe she wouldn't be so nervous this time. I had a feeling she might know Mr. Duffy better than anyone else I'd encountered so far. Duffy had bought children's clothes at the secondhand store. He had bought children's books at the library. He had stolen spices from a grocery store. And maybe all for that woman and her little girl.

My cell phone trilled *yet again*.

"I'll buy you a *box* of biscotti, Morgan," I said. "Just hang in a little longer—"

"He's a scrawny guy, right?" Morgan said. Her voice was hard to make out. "Dark hair, thin face, wearing a short jacket?"

"Morgan, I can hardly hear you."

Nothing.

"Morgan?" I peered up the street but didn't see her. "You still there?"

"He just went past me and got on a bus," Morgan said, her voice louder and clearer. "Night Owl Cleaners . . . do their jackets have a big yellow circle on them, owl in the center?"

"You have to ask?" I said.

"Must have been him."

"Did you see which house he came out of?"

"I sure did. And I heard what you said about a box of biscotti. I'm gonna hold you to it."

I hurried up the street to meet her. I had a bag in one hand.

"That's the place," Morgan said, pointing to a run-down, two-story brick house.

We climbed the rickety wooden steps and knocked on the door. No one answered. A man carrying two garbage bags appeared from around the side of the house. He glanced at us as he toted the bags to the curb. Then he disappeared around the side of the house again. He was back a minute later with a couple more bags. He paused and looked at us again.

"What's his problem?" Morgan said.

I knocked again, louder this time. Still no answer.

"The woman and the little girl must have gone out before I saw the man leave," Morgan said.

"Maybe," I said. I wished we'd started watching the street sooner.

"You girls looking for someone?" the man called to us from the curb.

"Someone needs a hobby," Morgan muttered.

"Maybe he knows her." I turned to the man. "We're looking for the woman who lives here."

He gave me a strange look. "There's six women who live here," he said. "Some guys, too. It's apartments. Knocking on that door"—he nodded at the front door—"won't do you any good." When we didn't move, he shook his head. "You have to go inside," he said, "and knock on the door of the person you're looking for."

Morgan opened the outer door and we stepped into a cramped lobby.

"This place doesn't look big enough for six apartments," Morgan said.

"They must be awfully small," I agreed.

Morgan looked around the bleak foyer. "So, which one are we looking for?"

I looked at the six mailboxes on the wall beside the door. Each one had a name printed on a little card taped to the top of the box. I pulled my wallet out of my bag and fished out the thrift store receipt that Ben and I had found in one of Mr. Duffy's books. One of the mailbox name cards had been printed in what looked like the same slender, elegant handwriting as the telephone number on the back of the receipt. I pointed to it.

"That one," I said. Mailbox number five. "Khan, R."

Morgan looked at the three doors that led off the tiny foyer. "Door number one, door number two, or door number three?" she said.

"Mailbox five. . . ." I said. "Let's try door three."

Door number three opened onto a flight of stairs that led to the second floor of the house. At the top were two more doors—apartments five and six. I knocked on the door to five. At first I saw light behind the peephole in the door. Then the peephole went dark, like someone's eye was pressed up against it. When it finally went light again, I thought the door would open. But it didn't. I knocked another time.

"No one's home," Morgan said. To my surprise, she actually sounded disappointed.

I knocked harder. The flimsy door rattled in its frame.

"Robyn, take a hint," Morgan said. "We'll have to come back another time."

The door opened an inch, startling Morgan, and a woman peeked out over the security chain.

"Hi," I said. "Remember me? I saw you at the funeral. I know you were a friend of Mr. Duffy's. I knew him too."

The woman looked at us. She shook her head and started to close the door. I pushed against it to keep it open.

"Please," I said. "I just want to talk to you for a few minutes."

"I must close the door before I can open it," the woman said.

The door shut, and I heard the rattle of the security chain. A moment later the door opened again.

The woman inside was small and slender. She had a blanket wrapped around her shoulders for warmth. A small, dark-eyed girl peeked out from behind her.

"You may come in," the woman said.

Morgan and I wiped our feet on the small mat outside the door before entering.

"How did you know where to find me?" the woman said.

Embarrassed, I explained that I had followed her. "But only because it's important," I said. I explained how I knew Mr. Duffy and that I was trying to find out more about him. "I feel partly responsible for what happened," I said.

The woman frowned. "You?" she said. "How are you responsible?"

I told her what had happened at the shelter, how Mr. Duffy had been banned just before one of the coldest nights of the year and how, because of that, he had frozen to death. The woman listened in silence. When I had finished, she said, "He was difficult to understand. How he acted, I mean. At first, he frightened me. But he never scared Yasmin. This is Yasmin." She laid a hand on the head of the little girl who clung to her. "I am Aisha. It is a cold night. Please, let me make you some tea."

We removed our boots and shucked our coats. I was glad that I had worn a warm sweater. The two small rooms that made up the tiny apartment were chilly. As I looked around the sparsely furnished place and remembered how underdressed for the weather she, her husband, and their little girl had been, I realized that buying flowers to take to the funeral must have been a real sacrifice.

"Please, sit," Aisha said, indicating a battered couch against one wall. She disappeared into the small room off the main room—the bathroom—to fill a kettle. She set the kettle on the small, battered stove and turned on a burner. While we waited for the water to boil, we found out a little more about Aisha and her husband Rashid.

They had recently immigrated from Pakistan, thinking that the move would offer more opportunities to Yasmin. They had been told before they left their home that they would have no trouble finding employment and had saved their money so that they would have enough to live on while they got settled. Rashid had been a civil engineer in Pakistan. Aisha had been a medical doctor. But neither had been able to find work in their field. Their qualifications weren't recognized. No one would hire Rashid because he didn't have any experience in this country. Before she could practice medicine again, Aisha would have to take new exams in order to qualify. And they couldn't afford that. As it was, she said, they had been in the country for nearly nine months and had used up almost all of their savings. It had taken Rashid nearly six months to find a job. He had worked in telemarketing for a few weeks, but hated it so much that Aisha had insisted he quit.

"Now he cleans offices at night," she said. "He does not like it. He feels it demeans him. But what can we do?"

Everything had turned out to be much more expensive than they had expected. And they, like everyone else, had been surprised at how early winter had come this year and at how cold it had been so far.

"There are stores where you can buy warm winter clothing secondhand," I said. "But they're clean and in good condition."

"Yes," she said. "I know. I have been to one. I bought a coat for Yasmin. But when Rashid found out that the store was operated by a charity, he made me take it back. He is very proud. He will not accept charity."

I thought about the clothing that Mr. Duffy had bought and then returned. It was starting to make sense.

The kettle started to whistle and Aisha hurried to the stove to make the tea. She poured it into delicate glass teacups that she had set out on a tray. The tea was milky and smelled sweet and fragrant.

I set my bag on the table and pulled out a box.

"We brought some cupcakes," I said. I'd been thinking of the little girl when I bought them. "Chocolate," I said, smiling at Yasmin. "Do you like chocolate?"

Yasmin nodded and watched me open the box. Her eyes grew big as she approached to look at the sweets inside. She turned to her mother. Aisha said something to her softly. She took three small plates from the cupboard over the stove. She put one of the cupcakes on a plate and handed it to Yasmin. The little girl sat on a chair and peeled off the paper, then broke off the bottom of the cupcake and ate it in small bites between sips of extra-milky tea, finally nibbling on the top half of the cupcake, which was covered with thick chocolate frosting.

Aisha insisted that Morgan and I each have a cupcake, but she didn't have one herself.

"About Mr. Duffy," I said at last.

"He was kind to us," Aisha said. "He tried to help us."

"Tried?" Morgan said.

"We met him in the park during the summer. That is to say, Yasmin met him." She looked fondly at her daughter. "She was playing. She ran across the park while I wasn't looking. All of a sudden, a big dog ran toward her and frightened her."

I looked sympathetically at Yasmin. The same thing had happened to me when I was small, except that the big dog I had encountered had bitten me, giving me a severe case of canine-phobia.

"Then a man—Mr. Duffy—came and took the dog by the collar. He returned it to its owner, who had not been paying attention. The man who owned the dog was very rude to Mr. Duffy. He said that his dog was harmless, that it had as much right to be in the park as anyone else. Mr. Duffy tried to tell him that the dog had frightened Yasmin, but the man wouldn't listen. He called Mr. Duffy names. He was rude to him. That made me very angry." Her eyes flashed. "When I told the man he should be more polite and he should take care of his dog, he became angry with me too. He called me names."

"I'm sorry," I said.

Aisha took a sip of her tea. "I thanked Mr. Duffy for helping Yasmin. He was very quiet. He kept his head down. He wouldn't look at me. I think the man with the dog made him feel ashamed of his appearance. His face—" She glanced at Yasmin. "If you didn't know him, he could look very fierce. I think he didn't want to frighten Yasmin the way the dog did. He walked away.

A few days later we saw him in the park again. It was still warm, and I had brought our lunch with us so that Yasmin and I could have a picnic.

"When I saw him, I wanted to thank him for helping Yasmin. I invited him to share our lunch. At first he didn't want to. But when Yasmin offered him some food, he finally accepted. He ate with real pleasure." She smiled proudly. "The next day we saw him again. He had a tin of preserved peaches with him. He wanted me to take it home, but I couldn't. Rashid would want to know where I had got it. If I told him that it was a gift from a stranger, he wouldn't let me keep it. Nor could I tell him that I had bought the peaches. He would want to know why I'd thrown away money on something like that. Mr. Duffy took the tin to a restaurant across the street from the park. When he came back, it was open and he had plastic spoons and we ate the peaches in the park—the whole tin! They were delicious." She smiled at the memory.

"After that, we often saw him in the park or on the street," she said. "He would sit on the street and people would give him money. I felt so sorry for him. But he always had something for us. For Yasmin. He liked to bring her cookies." I remembered the ones he had tried to steal from the homeless shelter.

"And spices," I said. "He gave you spices."

"How did you know?" Aisha said.

I told a little white lie. I said that a clerk in a grocery store had told me.

Aisha nodded. "He also bought warm clothing for us from one of those thrift stores. But I had to make him take it back. Rashid would never accept it. Mr. Duffy didn't understand that. He kept bringing things for Yasmin, and always I had to ask him to return them. One time when we were out with Rashid, we saw him and Yasmin ran to talk to him. Rashid didn't like that. He was like the man in the park—he only saw what Mr. Duffy looked like. I argued with him later, but it didn't do any good. Rashid can be very stubborn."

I took out the thrift store receipt with the phone number written on the back of it and the letter F next to it.

"Did you give him this number?" I said.

She nodded. "I know the woman who runs the laundromat. I do my laundry there every Friday."

"Is that what the F means?" I said.

"I told him he could reach me there on Fridays. Or he could leave a message for me there, in case anything happened and he needed something. I worried about him, especially in the cold weather. But he never telephoned. He never asked for help."

"Did Mr. Duffy ever talk about his personal life?" I said.

Aisha hesitated for a moment and then shook her head.

"Did you hear the young man who spoke at the funeral?" I said. She nodded. "He liked Mr. Duffy. And he thinks it's terrible that nobody knows anything about him. He thinks that unless he can tell Mr. Duffy's story—you know, let people know who he was before he ended up on the street, help them understand *how* he ended up on the street—that people will just go on thinking that homeless people aren't like the rest of us, that they deserve to be on the street because they're lazy or stupid or crazy."

"Mr. Duffy was not stupid," Aisha said. She sounded surprised that anyone would think such a thing. "He was very smart. I think he was a businessman before his life changed."

"What makes you think that?"

"He knew a lot. And he read a lot. He liked to go to the library."

"Did he ever talk about what kind of work he used to do?"

She shook her head.

"Did he ever tell you what happened to him, how he ended up on the street?"

She shook her head again.

"Sometimes he had terrible headaches," she said. "He'd had a bad injury. I asked him what had happened to him, but he never told me. Sometimes he didn't remember things."

Yasmin scampered back into the room. I hadn't even noticed that she had been gone. She tugged on her mother's tunic and said something softly that I couldn't understand. Then she pressed something into her mother's hand. Aisha sat silently for a moment, clutching whatever Yasmin had just given her, her eyes staring down at the threadbare carpet on the floor.

"I don't know where he came from," she said at last, looking up to meet my eyes. "But one day he said to me, 'Aisha, would *you* take me back?'"

"Back where?" Morgan said.

Aisha shrugged. "I asked him what he meant. But he just shook his head and said he was being foolish. He said probably he had imagined it, probably he was seeing things."

"Seeing what?" I said.

"I don't know. He got up and walked away after that. He didn't even say goodbye to Yasmin. I don't think he was feeling well."

"When did this happen?" I said.

"Not long ago. Maybe a week. The next day he gave me this. He asked me to keep it safe for him. He was always afraid someone would steal it from him. He said it was all he had." She opened her hand to reveal a ring and a small envelope. Then she opened the envelope and took out a small black-and-white photograph that had been trimmed into an oval shape. It was a picture of a boy, maybe sixteen or seventeen years old.

"Did he say who this is?" I said.

Aisha shook her head. "But it looks very old. I thought at first it was a picture of him, but it doesn't look anything like him."

It sure didn't. But then, this was the picture of a boy. Mr. Duffy had been over sixty years old when he died, according to the coroner's estimate. Morgan took the picture from me and peered at it.

"Some things never change," she said.

I looked at her. "What do you mean?"

"School pictures," she said. "They're like driver's license photos and passport photos. You always come out looking like either a geek or a criminal. This guy's definitely a geek—check the outfit." Even though the picture was small—just head and shoulders—we could make out a white shirt, a jacket, and a tie.

Aisha handed me the ring. It was a school ring. The words *St. Mark's Academy* were inscribed on it. There was no date.

"You can take these," Aisha said. "Maybe they will help you."

I slipped the ring and the envelope into my bag. Morgan and I put on our boots and coats while Aisha tidied up the tea things and retied the string on the cupcake box.

"Aisha?" I said. I held out the bag from the toy store—a gift for Yasmin. Aisha peeked into it but shook her head. I didn't argue with her. She handed me the remaining cupcakes.

"But the cupcakes are for you," Morgan protested.

I took the box from Aisha. "Thanks for your help," I said. "We really appreciate it." I fumbled in my purse until I found a piece of paper and a pen. I wrote down my phone number and handed it to her. "If there's anything I can do—if you need someone to babysit Yasmin, anything at all—call me. I mean it."

She nodded and folded the piece of paper, then tucked it into her pocket. "If you find out anything about Mr. Duffy, will you tell me?" she said.

I promised I would.

When we were outside again, Morgan said, "Now what?"

I looked down at the ring and the small envelope.

CHAPTER **ELEVEN**

Morgan and I parted company. She was going home. I was heading over to my father's place, but I decided to make a stop along the way.

The staff and volunteers at the shelter were gearing up for another out-of-the-cold night. They were busy setting up cots and laying out blankets and pillows in the main hall. The place was more crowded than usual. I had to thread my way through people and bedding to get to the far end of the hall, where I'd spotted Art Donovan talking to a client.

"Robyn," he said when he had finished his conversation. "I've already told Ben, and now I'm going to tell you."

"Tell me what?"

"That what you and Ben have been doing has resulted in some generous donations to our shelter."

"Really?" I had already given him the wad of twenties that the man outside the office building had given me.

"I received a thousand-dollar donation from a judge," he said. "And a man—a Mr. Franklin—wrote us an even bigger check. He mentioned you by name and said he thought what you were doing was admirable." I recognized the name. It was the man who had given me his business card. He'd told Ben and me to let him know if we ever solved our "little mystery." After hearing about his donation, I promised myself that I would do just that.

"That's great," I said. "Mr. Donovan, I was wondering—"

"Excuse me," someone said. A volunteer who was preparing to set up a couple more cots.

"We'd better step into my office," Art said.

We had to squeeze through more people to get there. Cots filled the main hall, and some had already been claimed. I was surprised by how many faces I recognized: Andrew, some of the men I'd seen outside smoking, the man who wore all of his clothes rather than risk being robbed, the man with the black stocking cap from the funeral, even Aggie, who scowled at me and muttered something angrily under her breath. She still hadn't forgiven me for contradicting her.

We went into Art's office, but he left the door ajar to keep an eye on the proceedings.

"What can I do for you, Robyn?"

I handed him the little oval photograph that Aisha had given me and watched as he studied it.

"Am I supposed to recognize this boy?" he said.

"Do you?" I said.

He examined the photo again. "You don't by any chance want me to say this looks like a young Mr. Duffy, do you?"

I felt a small surge of excitement. "Do you think it does?"

He shook his head slowly. "I'm sorry, but not to me it doesn't."

"And you've never seen this picture before?" I said.

"No."

"What about this ring?" I showed it to him. He shook his head again.

"I'm sorry, Robyn. I've never seen either of them before."

I had been hoping for a different answer, but I hadn't really been expecting one.

Betty gave me the same response. I looked around the main hall for Andrew.

"Do you recognize either of these?" I said, and showed him the photograph and the ring.

He inspected both items and shook his head. When he saw my expression, he gave me a sympathetic look. "Wrong answer, huh?"

"Well, it wasn't the one I was hoping for. Someone gave me these. They belonged to Mr. Duffy. I thought maybe they meant something." I glanced around. The place was really filling up. I wondered what the chances were that Mr. Duffy had shown the photo and the ring to anyone else.

"Do you want me to ask around for you?" Andrew said in his soft, mumbly voice. "People might tell me things that they wouldn't say to you."

"Would you?"

He started to smile, but quickly hid his mouth with his hand again.

He took the ring and the photo and began a circuit of the room. He spoke to everyone—the smokers, Aggie, the man with the black tuque, even the volunteers who were handing out blankets and pillows. Mostly I saw heads shaking in response to what he was saying. A few times, the person he was talking to turned and looked at me. Then, suddenly, a man grabbed the ring out of Andrew's hand and bolted for the door. Andrew ran after him and caught up just outside the front door. The man looked over Andrew's shoulder at me. It was the man with the mismatched eyes. He glowered at me just as he'd done the time I'd tried to ask him about Duffy. I heard Andrew mention the police. The man swore, but he thrust the ring at Andrew and stalked away. Andrew turned to come back inside.

"I don't like that guy," he said. "He's crazy. Always trying to take people's stuff."

We went back inside, and Andrew continued where he had left off. When he had finally spoken to every person in the room, he said, "Nobody knows anything." He sounded more disappointed than I was.

"Thanks for asking," I said. I slipped the ring and the photo into my coat pocket and said good night.

As usual, there was a small group of men on the sidewalk in front of the shelter. Most of them were smoking what looked like hand-rolled cigarettes. And, as usual, they ignored me—all except for the man with the mismatched eyes. He stared as I came down the steps. He looked fierce, but I told myself that it was just his strange eyes. I wrapped my hand around the ring and walked past him. As I started up the street for the bus stop, one of the shelter's vans turned into the church parking lot and unloaded more clients. Eileen got out with them. I doubled back and showed her the picture. She just shook her head. With a sigh, I headed back to the sidewalk. On my way I passed the man in the black stocking cap who had been at the funeral. I realized then that I had been wrong about him—he must have been a volunteer, not a client, because he got into a car and drove up the street past me.

The bus shelter was empty when I got there. It was dark and cold out, and I was tired and hungry. I glanced at my watch and then at the schedule posted on the glass. I'd just missed a bus and would have to wait ten minutes for the next one. I hugged myself and stamped my feet to stay warm.

Someone stepped into the bus shelter with me—the man with the mismatched eyes. He stared at me with his one good eye. Was he still after the ring? Did he think he could get it away from me now that I was all alone?

I closed my hand protectively around the ring and the photo in my pocket and glanced up and down the street, hoping to see someone, anyone, approaching the bus stop.

There was no one in sight, and the man kept staring.

At first I turned away and ignored him. Then he moved closer. I felt myself tense up. He moved even closer, blocking my exit. I saw the clouds of his breath in my peripheral vision. I decided to get out of there.

"Excuse me," I said. The man didn't move. I darted around behind him, squeezed out of the bus shelter, and walked quickly away. I told myself to stay calm. Andrew had said that the guy was crazy, but he hadn't said that he was dangerous. Maybe he was really just waiting for the bus. Then I looked back.

He was following me.

I walked a little faster.

I could hear his footsteps quicken too.

I glanced over my shoulder again. He was right behind me, and there was no one else around.

I spotted a car coming in my direction. A lit dome on the roof—a taxi.

I raised a hand to flag it down, and jumped in as soon as it pulled over. "Where to?" the taxi driver said.

I gave him my father's address.

. . .

When the taxi pulled up in front of my father's building, I told the driver that I would be right back, that I needed to get some money. But when I got out, the driver jumped out too and grabbed me by the arm. Maybe he hadn't understood me. Or maybe he was afraid I was trying to get away without paying him.

"I'll be right back," I told him again. But he wouldn't let me go.

Fortunately, Lauren, the hostess at La Folie, spotted me out on the sidewalk and went to get my dad, who was occupying his usual table for dinner. He ran out into the frigid night and paid my fare. Then he shepherded me back into the restaurant, where he had been enjoying an after-dinner cognac with his business partner, Vern Deloitte.

"We were just talking about you, Robyn," Vern said when I approached the table.

"You were?"

"Mac told me all about that homeless man who froze to death," Vern said. "Sounds like you've been doing some good. This is the season for it."

I nodded distractedly. I felt shaky all over and I couldn't stop myself from turning to look outside. I kept expecting to see the man with mismatched eyes.

"Robbie, are you okay?" my father said.

"Huh?"

He was staring intently at me. "You keep looking out the window. And you're shaking like a leaf."

"There was this man," I said. "He was following me. That's why I took a taxi over here."

My father's expression turned grim. "What man?" he said. "What do you mean, he was following you?" He got up and helped me pull my coat off. That's when I realized that my hand was still clenched around the ring and the small photo. I put them on the table and pulled off my gloves.

"I think he wanted this ring. He tried to steal it when Andrew was showing it around the homeless shelter."

My father looked at the ring and photo and frowned. "I think you'd better back up, Robbie. Whose ring is this, who is Andrew, and why was he showing it around?"

"Andrew is a regular at the shelter. He was showing it around to see if anyone had seen it before. Mr. Duffy gave it to someone for safekeeping. I was trying to find out if it was a picture of him."

"The man who froze to death," my father said to Vern.

Vern turned the photo his way. He glanced across the table at my father, their expressions both serious. Two ex-cops, their antennae up.

"Tell me about the man who followed you," my father said.

"After Andrew caught him and made him give back the ring, he followed me to the bus stop," I said. "He kept staring at me. He was making me nervous, so I started to walk away. He followed me again. That's when I flagged down a taxi."

I began to feel like I'd been nervous about nothing. "He was on foot," I said. "There's no way he could have followed me here. He scared me, Dad. But I'm okay now."

I sensed my father relaxing just a little. Vern drained the cognac from his glass and stood up.

"You want me to check the guy out, Mac?" he said.

My father shook his head. "I think Robbie's right. If he was on foot, he couldn't have followed her. I think we're in the clear for now."

"Okay," Vern said. "You take care of yourself, now, Robyn. And I think what you're doing is great. I mean it."

I thanked him. I really like Vern. He's kind of like an uncle to me. He's known me my whole life, and he's always as proud of me as my parents are.

"Call me if you need me, Mac," he said.

"Have you had dinner, Robbie?" my father said after Vern left.

I shook my head.

My dad flagged down a waiter. While we waited for my order, he asked me what happened.

I told him exactly how the ring and the photo had come into my possession and how I had gone back to the shelter to see if anyone recognized them. By the time I had finished my story, my heart had stopped pounding and my hands and feet no longer felt like blocks of ice. The waiter arrived with my food. As I plowed into it, my father picked up the ring and looked closely at it.

"It's a school ring," he said. "There used to be a St. Mark's Academy here in town. A boys' school."

"Used to be? It doesn't exist anymore?" I had been hoping the school would be able to help me find out something about Mr. Duffy—assuming he had ever been a student there.

"It went co-ed about twenty years ago and changed its name. I think it's called the Ashdale Academy now."

"Ashdale Academy? But Ashdale *is* an all-boys' school, Dad."

"The co-ed thing didn't work out. It reverted to boys-only after a couple of years. You're sure this belonged to Mr. Duffy?"

"He gave it and the photo to Aisha for safekeeping," I said. "They must have meant something to him."

My father examined the photograph. "That's kind of an old-fashioned haircut. And that tie . . . I'd say this was taken forty, maybe fifty years ago. You think it could be Duffy when he was young?"

"I was hoping," I said. "But no one who knew Mr. Duffy sees any resemblance."

"It's cut in an odd shape, don't you think?"

I had wondered about the shape. It looked like someone had trimmed it—maybe to fit a locket.

My dad's phone rang.

"Excuse me a minute, Robbie."

"No problem." The truth was, I wanted to make a call myself. I pulled out my own phone and punched in Ben's number. He sounded surprised to hear from me. He sounded even more surprised when I asked him if there was any chance his school was open during the next week or if it had already closed for the holidays.

"It's closed," he said. When I sounded disappointed, he said, "Well, classes are over. Most of the teachers are probably gone. But I know there are still a few people around. I'm going over there tomorrow morning to pick up some stuff for the toy drive."

"Toy drive?"

"Ashdale and another school do a joint toy drive every year—you know, for underprivileged kids. I'm supposed to pick up the toys Ashdale collected and take them to the other school for the wrap-a-thon."

"Wrap-a-thon, huh? Do you think anyone will be in the office?"

"Well, I know Mr. Thorson is going to be there. He's the principal. Why?"

"What time are you going?"

"First thing."

"Can I meet you?"

"What's going on, Robyn?"

"I think I may have a lead, Ben. At least, I hope so. I'll show you tomorrow."

We agreed to meet in front of Ben's school at nine the next morning.

After I put my phone away, I ate every bite of my supper and told my father what Morgan and I had found out so far about Mr. Duffy.

"I'm impressed," he said, smiling at me. "Don't tell your mother, but if you ever decided to go into policing, you'd make detective in no time. You're a natural."

I grinned. "Everything I learned, I learned from you, Dad."

"Don't tell your mother that, either."

His phone rang again.

"Tara," he said into it, sounding pleased. "No, don't apologize. What can I do for you?"

Tara? If he was making plans with her, I didn't want to get in the way.

"I gotta go, Dad." I stood up.

"Just a moment," my father said into the phone. Then he looked up at me. "Go? Go where?"

"Home."

My father gave me an odd look. "Home?" he said. "I thought you were staying here tonight."

"I left something . . . um . . . I should go home, Dad." I scooped up the ring and the photograph and put them safely in my purse.

"Give me a minute and I'll drive you," my father said.

"It's okay. I can get there on my own."

"Well, at least let me give you cab fare." He pressed some bills into my hand. "Take a taxi. I insist. Have Lauren call one for you."

"Dad, stop worrying."

But I took the money and slipped on my coat while he resumed his phone conversation. When I got to the front of the restaurant, Lauren was busy seating a large group of diners who had just arrived. I didn't want to bother her.

It was quiet out on the street. A couple of cars went by, but no taxis. I decided to walk down to the intersection, where there was more traffic. I was a block away from the restaurant when I felt a sharp jerk on my purse strap. Then the purse fell away from my shoulder. The strap had been cut. I started to turn around and got shoved into a dark alley. Whoever pushed me was wearing a balaclava so that I couldn't see his face. He was holding a knife. I stared at it and couldn't make myself look away. The blade was long and looked razor-sharp.

CHAPTER TWELVE

I opened my mouth. I don't think I was going to scream. I'm pretty sure that I understood it would be crazy to make any noise at all under the circumstances. But I opened my mouth anyway, and I think that's what made him hit me. I fell to the ground, stunned but not unconscious. I felt rough hands plunging into my pockets, yanking things out. Then he pushed me down again, on my stomach this time. I lay there for a moment, too frightened to move.

I peered around.

The man was gone.

I staggered to my feet and touched the bandage that hid my stitches, afraid that he had reopened the wound on my face. But it was dry. My phone lay on the ground at my feet. I picked it up and put it back into my pocket. The money my father had given me was gone. I wobbled back to La Folie.

My father was still talking on the phone, but he ended his call the moment he saw me. The expression on his face told me that I looked as shaky as I felt. He put his arms around me and led me out the door and up the stairs to his place. He made me tell him everything. When I had finished, he made a phone call. It wasn't long before two uniformed police officers arrived, and my dad made me tell them what I had already told him.

"What about that bandage on your face. Is that from the man who robbed you?" one of the cops said.

I shook my head and explained the stitches.

"Do you think the man who robbed you outside the restaurant is the same man who followed you to the bus shelter?"

"I don't know. I didn't get a good look at him."

"He was wearing a balaclava," my father said grimly.

"What about the man from the bus shelter?" the same cop said. "Can you describe him?"

I nodded and told them everything I remembered. They wrote down the description and asked me some more questions about what I had seen when I left the restaurant before they shut their notebooks. My father followed the officers to the door and talked to them for a few minutes before they finally left.

"They're going to check out the guy who followed you to the bus shelter," my father said. He caught my chin in one hand and tilted my head back so that he could get a good look at me. "You're going to have a bruise," he said. His fog-gray eyes held mine. "I should have driven you to your mother's."

"When I saw that knife—"

"It's okay, Robbie. You're safe now." He reached for my coat. "Come on. I'll take you home."

"But what if the police find out something?"

"If they do, I'll let you know."

"What if they want to talk to me again?"

"Then *they'll* let you know."

"If they call me at Mom's, Mom will freak out. She'll never let me come down here alone again."

"Robbie, your mother has a right to know—"

"She's already been giving me a hard time about the homeless shelter. Please, Dad. I'm okay, really. We don't have to upset her, do we?"

He was still holding my coat, but he didn't try to help me into it.

"You have to tell her."

"She already knows I was planning to spend the night here."

"Didn't you say you left something at home?"

"It's not important," I said. "Please, Dad. You know how she can be."

My father hesitated.

"You have to *promise* me that you'll tell her what happened when you see her," he said at last. "When she sees that bruise—"

"I'll tell her, I promise. But not tonight. Okay, Dad?"

Finally, reluctantly, he agreed.

I took a long, hot bath and then curled up in front of the TV. I had almost given up hope of hearing from the police again that night when my father's buzzer sounded. He went to answer it. A few moments later, he opened the door and the same two officers stepped in. One of them was holding my purse, its strap cut in half and dangling uselessly.

"Where did you find it?" I said.

"In an alley a couple of blocks away," he said. "That's pretty standard. Purse snatchers grab a purse and run like hell. When they think they're safe, they take everything of value and dump the purse. Your wallet's inside. But we're going to want to hold onto it for a while. It's evidence. Same with your wallet. We'll see if we can get some prints off them."

"But he was wearing gloves," I said. "The guy who attacked me was wearing gloves."

"Purse snatchers aren't exactly geniuses," the cop said. "You'd be surprised how many guys wear gloves when they're doing the crime and then do something stupid right after, like taking off the gloves so they can go through the purse easier. It's always worth checking. We'll let you know if we find anything. I can give you back your ID—but you'll have to sign for it. Did you have any money in the wallet?"

I nodded.

"Well. I hope it wasn't much. It's gone now," the cop said. "Credit cards?"

I shook my head.

"Anything else of value?"

"There was a gold ring in the purse. And a photograph. Are they still there?"

The cop shook his head.

"Are you sure?"

"Positive. I inventoried the contents myself." He showed me the list he had written.

"There are other things missing," I said. "Some lip gloss. Some blush."

"It's possible he tossed those," the cop said.

"Maybe he threw away the ring, too," I said. "Or the photo."

What would a purse snatcher want with an old photograph? I wondered.

I spoke up again. "Where exactly did you find my purse?"

When he described the alley, my father nodded. "I know the one you mean."

"We found the purse about halfway down," the cop said. "The place is a mess. It's possible your makeup is in there somewhere. Maybe the picture, too. But a gold ring? I doubt it, but we can take another look."

"It's okay," my father said. "I'll do it myself."

The cop nodded. He reached into his pocket and pulled out a Polaroid photo. "Is this the guy who followed you from the shelter to the bus stop?"

I looked at the man in the photo. He had one dark eye and one milky white eye.

"That's him."

"Well, he wasn't the guy who attacked you downstairs," the cop said. "The director at the shelter says this guy went out for a smoke early in the evening—just about the time you left to walk to the bus stop. He was back fifteen minutes later and stayed inside for the rest of the night."

"He's sure about that?" my father said.

"He's positive. So is the woman who works in the kitchen. A bunch of other people at the place say he was there all evening." The two cops stood up. "We're going to check your purse and wallet for prints. If we find any, we'll run them against what's in the system."

The second cop, who had stayed silent and had done most of the note-taking, returned my ID, my library card, my transit card. He made me sign for each item. Then the two cops left.

"How about a cup of tea?" my father said.

I slipped on my boots and my coat. "Show me where that alley is?"

"Robyn, it's nearly midnight. Whatever's there is going to stay there, believe me."

"Please, Dad? If the ring is there, I don't want to take the chance that someone will find it. It could be important. You don't have to go with me if you don't want to." But I sure hoped that he *would* want to. "Just tell me where it is." I buttoned my jacket and pulled on my gloves.

My father sighed and stood up. "You are so stubborn," he said. "Sometimes I don't know who you remind me more of—your mother or me."

He pulled on his snow gear and got a couple flashlights out of a drawer. We trudged down the street to the alley the two police officers had described and spent nearly an hour hunting through the trash cans, discarded boxes, and scraps of litter. I found my blusher. My father found my lip gloss. But we didn't find the ring or the photo.

. . .

After a nearly sleepless night, I met Ben the next morning. He was waiting for me on the sidewalk in front of a modern-looking building in one of the most upscale parts of the city. The weather hadn't changed. It was still bone-shatteringly cold out. I had a hat pulled down over my ears and a thick wool scarf wrapped around my neck and chin. I stared up at the glass-and-steel structure.

"*This* is Ashdale Academy?" I had heard of it, but I had never seen it.

"What were you expecting?" Ben asked. "Gothic towers and ivory-covered walls?"

"Something like that," I admitted. I'd at least been expecting something a lot older. "My dad must have made a mistake. He said that this school used to be called St. Mark's."

"It did."

"Well, there must be more than one. The school I'm looking for was around at least forty or fifty years ago." If Mr. Duffy had gone there, it would have been much,

much older than the school I was staring at. "This place looks like it was built way more recently."

"It was," Ben said. "This building was supposed to be an addition to the original St. Mark's."

"Supposed to be?"

"There was a fire," Ben said. "Shortly after the new wing was built."

"A fire?"

"They had to knock down the old building completely. Expand the new addition. My father helped to raise the money for it. What are we doing here, Robyn? You said you had a lead on Mr. Duffy."

When I'd talked to him the night before, I had imagined presenting him with the photo and the ring. But they were long gone. All I could do was tell him about them instead.

"Great work," he said. "Can I see them?"

"I'm afraid not. They were stolen."

His eyes widened. "Stolen?"

"I was mugged last night."

"*Mugged?* Were you hurt?"

I turned my head and pulled down my scarf so he could see the bruise on my face.

His eyes widened even more. "Are you okay?"

"I'm fine." At least I was *by then*. I had thought I was fine at my father's last night, too, after the police left. But I'd had trouble falling asleep. I tossed and turned and twisted the sheets into knots. I kept thinking about that knife.

"Did you call the police? Did they catch the guy who mugged you?"

"Yes," I said. "But no, they didn't. Not yet, anyway."

"You think the ring means that Duffy used to go to St. Mark's?" he said.

It was hard to imagine. "Maybe. Or maybe somebody important to him did. But he told Aisha that he didn't want to lose the ring or the picture, so they must have been valuable to him."

I shivered as a gust of wind hit me.

"Do you think we could go inside?" I asked.

Ben nodded. He led the way up the walk and rang a bell beside the front door. I peered inside. The school looked deserted except for a man who was mopping the floor just inside the main doors. He looked up when he heard the buzzer and came and opened the door for us.

"Hi Pete," Ben said, standing aside to let me go in first.

"Ben, didn't they tell you?" Pete said, grinning at him. "School's out for the holidays."

"I'm here to pick up the toys for the toy drive," Ben said.

Pete gestured to a huge pile of cardboard cartons stacked to one side of the lobby.

"I'll go get a dolly," he said. "It'll go faster that way."

"Thanks," Ben said. "I'll meet you back here in a few minutes. I need to talk to Mr. Thorson. Have you seen him?"

"Who do you think packed all those boxes?" Pete said. "He's in the office."

"Come on," Ben said.

I followed him down the hallway to the school's offices. Like the rest of the school, they were silent and empty. Well, almost empty.

"Ben," said the office's sole occupant, a smiling, bald-headed man dressed in gray slacks and a pullover sweater. He seemed as delighted to see Ben as Pete had been. "I put the toys in the lobby for you. Do you need help loading them up?"

"Pete's going to help me," Ben said. "But thanks anyway, Mr. Thorson."

Thorson's eyes moved from Ben to me. Ben took the hint and introduced us.

"Robyn and I were hoping you could give us some information," he said. "Robyn found a ring that she thinks might be from this school—from when it used to be St. Mark's."

"Hmm. May I see it?" Thorson said.

"I don't have it anymore," I said. "It was stolen last night."

"Oh?"

"But I can describe it," I said. I told him everything I could remember about the ring. But it wasn't until I did a rough sketch of the crest on its face that he started to nod. He got up, went to the wall behind his desk, and removed a framed certificate.

"Did it look like this?" he said, pointing to the crest that was embossed on the heavy certificate paper.

"Exactly," I said.

"Sounds as though it *was* a St. Mark's school ring," Thorson said. "As I understand it, that was the ring from the time the school opened until it changed its name, and that's twenty years ago now. I started as headmaster here the same year."

So my dad had been right after all. And if this was the right school, there was a chance that Mr. Duffy had been a student here. If he had, there would be records somewhere that could tell us something about him. Assuming, of course . . .

"Ben said the original school burned down," I said.

"That's right. Quite spectacularly," Thorson said. "A pity, too. The original building was over one hundred years old. We were able to incorporate some of what was left into the new building—a blend of the old and the new, bridging generations, as it were. Fortunately the new building was completed and renovations were just about to begin on the old structure, so we were able to carry on without missing a beat."

"What about the school records?" I said.

"We only lost the old records—everything dating back more than ten years before the new school opened," Thorson said.

My heart sank. "We were hoping there would be records on whoever the ring belonged to," I said.

"How old was he?" Thorson said.

"Sixty, maybe sixty-five."

Thorson shook his head. "I'm afraid anything that dates from that era is long gone."

"Was there a date on the ring, Robyn?" Ben said.

I shook my head.

"The St. Mark's school rings didn't have dates on them," Thorson said. "The graduation rings, which did, were of a different design. From the description you just gave me, I'd say that what you had was a school ring, not a graduation ring. Every boy who went to St. Mark's received one. There must be thousands in existence. As I understand it, the design of that ring never changed."

So no way to trace it to a specific graduating class, let alone a student, I thought.

"What about the photo?" Ben said.

"What photo?" Thorson said.

"I had a photo of a boy," I said. "It looked like a school picture. It was stolen along with the ring. But I'm pretty sure I'd recognize the face if I saw it again." That gave me an idea, but before I could say anything, Thorson shook his head.

"You're thinking that if you looked through old yearbooks, you might be able to find the same face. Well, I'm sorry, Robyn," Thorson said. "But that won't be possible, either."

"You mean there are no yearbooks?" Ben said, disappointed.

"Only Ashdale yearbooks. All the St. Mark's yearbooks are long gone," Thorson said.

"Were they burned in the fire too?" I said.

"Water-damaged. In a separate incident, believe it or not," Mr. Thorson said. "They were stored in the basement of the new school, this building you're standing in now. We had some problems with the pipes the first year. The basement flooded. Everything down there, including our collection of old yearbooks, was utterly destroyed. We were hoping some of our alumni would donate their personal copies so that we could rebuild our collection, but—" He shrugged. "I guess after a fire and a flooded basement, they didn't want to take any chances."

"So there's no way we can find out who the ring belonged to?"

Thorson looked genuinely apologetic. "I'm sorry," he said.

. . .

I helped Ben and Pete load the boxes of toys into the van Ben was driving. Then Ben dropped me at the bus stop before delivering the toys to their next destination.

"For a while I thought we really were on to something there," Ben said as I moved to let myself out. "Talk about bad luck, huh?"

"Well, it was worth a try," I said.

I went back to my father's place. It was still early. Morgan wouldn't be up yet, so I planned to just chill until it was time to go out again. I had promised to help out at the shelter in the afternoon.

When I unlocked the door, I heard music coming from my father's office.

"Dad?" I dropped my coat and my bag on a chair and went to see what he was doing.

He wasn't in the office, but Tara was. She was working on my dad's computer, so immersed in whatever she was doing that she didn't even seem to notice that I was there. I knocked on the door to get her attention. She jumped and spun around in her chair as if I'd jabbed her with a pin.

"Robyn," she said, her hand pressed to her chest. "You startled me."

"I was looking for my dad," I said. I stared at the computer screen and at the image that filled most of it. My mother's face. I crossed to the desk so that I could take a closer look. There was something weird about it—definitely my mom, but like no picture of her that I had ever seen. It just seemed off.

"Mac said he had to meet somebody," Tara said. She glanced at her watch and seemed surprised. "No wonder I'm hungry." She looked at me again. "I tend to get a little too involved in what I'm doing."

"What *are* you doing?" I said. What I really meant: Why is my mother's face on the computer? Supplementary question: Whatever you're doing, why are you doing it in my father's office?

"I'm working on age progression. My computer crashed, oh, two weeks ago now. It's still in the shop, can you believe it? Anyway, your father was nice enough to offer me the use of his. Ten times better than my old hunk of junk."

"Age progression? You mean, like the police do when they're trying to find some kid who disappeared years ago?"

"Missing kids, criminals at large, you name it." She nodded at the computer screen. "I've been practicing on some photos your father gave me, pictures of people he knows." She fumbled around on the desk until she found a photograph that I recognized instantly. A school picture of my mother, from when she was about ten years old. She showed me another photo—a geeky-looking Ted, age maybe thirteen or fourteen, which explained the image of him that I had seen on my father's computer earlier. I wondered where my dad had got the picture and if my mother knew that he had it. "I've been ageing them. Your dad has been able to tell me how well I'm doing because he knows what they look like now."

"Are you a cop?"

"I'm an anthropologist. My area is human osteology. That's—"

"The study of human bones. I know."

She nodded. "Thanks to one of my former professors, I've done a little work for the police. Identifying bones, giving the police some idea of how old they are, that sort of thing. I found it interesting, so I've been taking some courses. Age progression fascinates me."

"Oh." I looked at the image of my mother on the computer screen. "Um. You and my father. Are you—"

What was the right way to ask the question I had in mind?

Tara frowned. "Are we what?" Then a look of horror swept across her face. "You mean, are we . . . ?" She shook her head vigorously. "I'm in town to take a course, do some hands-on study with a forensic artist here. *The* expert in age progression and regression. Mac's been nice enough to show me around, and he offered me the use of his computer when mine crashed. But—"

She seemed mortified at the thought that I'd read more than that into the situation. "I mean, my God," she said. "I've known him my whole life as *Uncle* Mac. It's hard enough to get used to calling him just plain *Mac*, let alone . . ." She shook her head again.

"*Uncle* Mac?" I said.

"Your dad and my dad worked together."

I looked at her with new interest. "Your dad's a cop?"

"He was," she said. "He was killed in the line of duty twenty years ago."

"I'm sorry," I said.

She shrugged. "I was seven when it happened. My mother completely fell apart. Your dad and some of the other cops who worked with my father used to come around to check on her, do things around the house for her, take my brother and me out." She smiled. "I had more uncles than anyone I knew. And your dad was the nicest one. He always kept in touch with Brad— my brother—and me, even after Mom remarried a few years later and we moved across the country. I think that's one of the reasons I'm interested in this area of work—carrying on the family tradition. Brad didn't want anything at all to do with police work. He's a carpenter now."

I wondered why my father hadn't told me about Tara. Then I remembered what he'd said when I mentioned that she seemed a little young. "I think she's just about right," he had replied. Just about right to be the daughter of an old friend. He'd been having some fun with me. Maybe he'd been hoping I would tell my mother.

"I was going to make myself a cup of tea," I said. "Would you like one?"

Tara beamed at me. "I'd love one," she said.

On the way to the kitchen I checked my father's phone. There were no messages. Still no word from Nick.

CHAPTER **THIRTEEN**

The homeless shelter served a Christmas dinner every year that attracted more than two hundred and fifty people. Turkey, mashed potatoes, stuffing, gravy, rolls, and, for dessert, pie and ice cream. A local bakery donated the pies. Everything else was made at the shelter. Some of it—the gravy, the stuffing, the potatoes—could be prepared ahead of time and frozen or refrigerated. It was a lot of work. Betty needed all the help she could get to be ready in time for Christmas. I hung up my coat, changed out of my boots and into a pair of sneakers, and went to the kitchen to see what she wanted me to do.

"Onions," Betty said. "I need someone to chop onions." She nodded at a large bag sitting on the floor.

"How many do you need chopped?" I said.

"All 'em."

I heaved the sack of onions up onto the counter beside a cutting board and set to work. To my surprise, a few minutes later, Andrew set up beside me. He started to cut day-old loaves of bread into small cubes for the stuffing.

"Hey Robyn," he said, smiling at me without showing his teeth.

"Hey Andrew," I said. "Don't tell me they're making you work for your supper."

"I volunteered," he said. He looked proud of himself. "It's the thing to do this time of year, right?"

"Right," I said. Once again I wondered what had drawn Andrew to the street.

"Wow, that's a lot of onions," said a voice behind me. I whirled around. Ben was carrying a stack of bakery boxes. "Where do you want these, Betty?"

"I cleared out some space in one of the downstairs freezers," Betty said. "We'll freeze them until Christmas Eve. Robyn, do you think you could help Ben with those?"

I was glad to.

"You didn't tell me *you* were coming here today," I said.

"You didn't tell me you were coming."

It took us two trips to get all the pies downstairs and stacked in one of the shelter's mammoth chest freezers. There were forty boxes in all—twenty apple pies and twenty cherry pies. After we finished, Ben helped me chop onions. Then, under Betty's directions, we mixed a huge batch of bread stuffing. When we'd done everything that Betty had on her schedule for the day, Ben offered to drive me home.

. . .

"You live *here*?" he said. We were sitting in his car outside my father's place.

"My dad does. Why?"

"La Folie is supposed to be a really good. My dad comes here a lot. Does your father own it?"

I shook my head. "The building, but not the restaurant."

"So he's in real estate?"

"He has a private security company. He used to be a cop."

Ben looked impressed. "My father manufactures and sells bathroom fixtures," he said and shook his head. "It must be pretty exciting having a dad who's a cop."

"*Was* a cop," I said. "He was hardly ever home when I was little. He was always working. And when he was home, he hardly ever talked about what he did. So it wasn't *all* that exciting."

"Yeah, well, my dad *does* talk about his business," Ben said. "Believe me, I know more about bathroom fixtures than I ever wanted to—more than *anyone* should have to know. So, Billy told me you got arrested in the summer. Something about an animal rights protest?"

"I got arrested trying to stop *Billy* from getting arrested."

"Now *that* sounds exciting."

"Obviously you've never been arrested."

"I've never even known anyone who's been arrested." He smiled at me. "You know, I was wrong about you. You're not anything like the girls at St. Mildred's."

"That's the second time you've mentioned the girls at St. Mildred's. Do boys from Ashdale have an exclusive with girls from St. Mildred's or something?"

"St. Mildred's is our sister school," Ben said. "Apparently it was some big tradition for guys from St. Mark's to go out with girls from St. Mildred's. Now a lot of guys from Ashdale go out with girls from St. Mildred's."

"Rich boys dating rich girls, huh?"

Ben shrugged. "I guess. My mom went to St. Mildred's. My dad went to St. Mark's. They met while they were at school."

My eyes must have lit up, because he said, "I thought of that too. But my dad's at least fifteen years younger than Mr. Duffy. Their pictures wouldn't be in the same yearbook. And that's assuming that the ring actually belonged to Duffy. He could have found it—or stolen it. Besides, you said the picture didn't look anything like him."

I sighed and pushed open the car door. "Thanks for the lift."

"Robyn?"

I turned back around.

"You want to go out sometime? See a movie or something?"

"What?" I guess I sounded too surprised. Ben's face turned red and he stared at the steering wheel. "What I mean is, are you sure that's allowed?"

He looked blankly at me.

"I don't go to St. Mildred's," I said. "I don't even go to private school. The way you talk about those St. Mildred's girls, I thought they had dibs on you Ashdale boys. You know—like father, like son."

His expression turned grim. "I'm not anything like my father," he said. He looked down at the steering wheel again and drew in a deep breath. "So, how about it?"

"I'd like that," I said. I don't think I would have admitted it—especially not to Morgan—but I was really starting to like him. He was nice—well, he was if he didn't think you were a two-four. He was cute. He cared about other people. And he didn't seem like the kind of person who would take off without any warning.

I dug in my purse for paper and a pen and wrote out my number for him. "Call me," I said as I got out of the car. I had just turned to go into my father's building when a thought occurred to me. I ran back and knocked on Ben's window. "Girls from St. Mildred's and boys from Ashdale, do they go out with each other because they already know each other?"

"Sometimes," Ben said. "Why?"

"If they don't already know each other, how do they get together? Meet each other?"

Ben shrugged. "Through mutual acquaintances. School events. You know, the same way anyone meets anyone else."

"My school is co-ed. Guys meet girls in class or in clubs or in the hallway."

Ben laughed. "Okay, so we don't meet that way. People just meet people—you know, through friends, or just around. Plus, our schools have some joint events, like they did in the old days—although not exactly for the same reasons."

"What do you mean?"

"My mother told me that in her mom's time, and even in her time, St. Mark's and St. Mildred's used to organize dances and stuff specifically so that girls from St. Mildred's would meet boys from St. Mark's and get married someday. You should see the pictures in both her and my father's yearbooks. They're filled with guys in suits, arm in arm with girls in formal dresses."

I knew exactly the kind of picture he was talking about. And that gave me an idea.

"St. Mildred's didn't ever burn down, did it?"

"Not that I know of," Ben said.

When I told him my idea, he slapped his forehead. "I should have thought of that," he said.

I glanced at my watch. "You think there'd be anyone at St. Mildred's now?"

Ben shook his head. "I doubt it." When I looked disappointed, he said, "But there will be on Monday. And I can get us in."

"You can?"

He grinned. "I'll pick you up."

I spent the next day doing what Morgan liked to do best—Christmas shopping. By the end of the day we had both checked off almost everyone on our lists.

"Who do you have left?" she said.

"My mom," I said. She was always the last person on my list. I never knew what to get her, and she never gave me any hints.

"What about Nick? What did you get him?"

I felt a twinge of anger.

"Nothing," I said. "What would I do with a present if I got him one?"

"Still no word, huh?"

"Don't you think I would have told you, Morgan?" I said.

She looked offended.

"Sorry," I said. "I didn't mean to snap at you. It's not your fault."

Ben picked me up just before noon, and we drove to St. Mildred's.

"You sure someone will be there?" I asked on the way.

"Positive. I'm supposed to help deliver all the wrapped toys to the nonprofit we sponsor."

"You're supposed to go to St. Mildred's to pick up toys that students at *Ashdale* collected?" I was confused.

"You know how I told you that Ashdale does the toy drive every year with another school?" Ben asked. "Well, we do it with St. Mildred's. It's another tradition. I brought the toys Ashdale collected here yesterday and spent a couple of hours wrapping them."

We tried the main door. Locked. Ben pressed the buzzer, and we shivered as we waited for someone to answer. I glanced at Ben, who rocked back and forth on his feet, humming quietly to himself.

Nothing happened.

Ben continued to rock and hum.

Then I saw someone inside the school foyer. A man in work overalls. He shuffled toward the main door and peered out. He broke into a smile when he saw Ben and reached for a massive key ring that was attached to his belt. He looked familiar.

"Isn't that the janitor from *your* school?" I said to Ben.

"Yeah. He works at Ashdale and Mildred's."

"Hey Ben," Pete said, pushing the door open to admit us. We stepped into a richly paneled entrance hall. "Come back to help the ladies?"

"Are they still here?" Ben said.

"They're almost finished. They'll be ready to pack everything up soon," Pete said. "They're in the library."

"Thanks, Pete," Ben said. "You remember my friend Robyn?" Pete glanced at me and nodded. "She's helping me with something to do with Mr. Duffy. We want to look at old school yearbooks while we're here."

Pete looked confused. "What's Duffy got to do with yearbooks?"

"We're not sure," Ben said. "We're not even sure we're on the right track. But if we find out anything, we'll let you know."

Ben seemed to know the school well. He led me to the library.

"From the way Pete talked," I said, "I got the impression he knew Mr. Duffy."

"He did," Ben said. "Up until a few months ago, Pete was homeless. I met him at the shelter. He had some problems in the past. He was sick. You know, mentally ill. Things were pretty tough for him for a few years. When I met him, he was trying to get back on his feet. He was taking some job readiness courses at one of the community centers. He has a degree in chemistry."

"Really?"

"You're surprised, right?"

It would have been more accurate to say that I was stunned. I was as surprised to find out that Pete had a chemistry degree as I had been to learn that Mr. Duffy read Dickens and computer magazines. I was beginning to think that I needed to be more open-minded.

"He worked hard to get into college," Ben said. "He worked hard while he was there. Now he's working hard to get it all back. When I met him, he was willing to do anything to make enough money so that he could get his own place and start to get his life together again. So when I heard that Ashdale was looking for a part-time janitor—" He shrugged again.

"You helped him get the job?" I said.

"I talked to Mr. Thorson. He knew I was volunteering at the shelter. He said he'd interview Pete if he applied for the job, but he couldn't make any promises. Pete did really well in the interview. Mr. Thorson was impressed. He even arranged for Pete to sit in on some college lectures—you know, so he could start to get back on his original career track. And when St. Mildred's needed someone part-time, Mr. Thorson put in a word for him."

No wonder Pete always seemed so delighted to see Ben.

As soon as Ben opened the library door, a dozen heads turned in our direction. Several library tables had been pushed together. They were stacked with brightly wrapped Christmas gifts. A group of women were busily packing the gifts into large cardboard boxes, also decorated with Christmas gift wrap.

"Hi Ben!" someone called. It was a girl, our age. She was dressed in casual but expensive-looking clothes. The moment she spotted Ben, she hurried over to greet him, calling back over her shoulder, "Mom, Ben's here."

"Jess, hi," Ben said. Jess threw her arms around him and kissed him on both cheeks. Ben didn't look the least bit embarrassed. When Jess finally released him, he introduced me. Jess tossed me a "Hi" but didn't take her eyes off Ben for a second. "Jess is the head of student council at St. Mildred's," Ben said. "She's in charge of the toy drive."

A woman came over to us. She was as sleek as Jess but more elegantly dressed.

"Ben, right on time," she said warmly. "We're just finishing up." Once again Ben introduced me. The older woman greeted me politely but coolly and then turned to her daughter. "Let's start taking the boxes out to Ben's van."

"Come on, Ben," Jess said. She looped one of her arms through one of his and smiled up at him.

"I'll be right back," Ben said to me. "This won't take long."

I offered to help and followed Ben and Jess over to a table that was piled high with boxes. Another woman greeted Ben warmly.

"I heard you were here yesterday, Ben. I was sorry I missed you," this woman said. She began rooting around in an enormous handbag. Finally, she produced a small bundle of what looked like brochures. "We're raising money for a new computer lab," she said. "We've recruited one of our alums to be honorary chair of our fundraising committee. I was thinking that your father might be interested in this project. After all, your mother was a St. Mildred's graduate, wasn't she?" Ben nodded, but he no longer looked cheerful. "Would you would mind giving this to your father?" she said. "It's about the fundraising appeal. Tell him I'd be happy to discuss it with him after the holidays."

Ben accepted a brochure but stuffed it into his pocket without glancing at it. He seemed relieved when Jess's mother clapped her hands to get everyone's attention.

"All right, everyone," she announced. "Let's load up and get out of here."

The women pulled on coats and boots, and we each grabbed a box of toys. Pete joined us. The students and alumni at St. Mildred's and Ashdale had collected so many toys that it took three trips to load everything into Ben's van. Jess stuck close to Ben the whole time, her brown eyes sparkling as she chatted with him about her plans for Christmas and New Year's. He responded affably. When we had loaded the last of the boxes into the van and Jess's mother had climbed into her luxury SUV, Jess went up on tiptoes and kissed Ben again, on one cheek this time.

"See you at Stephanie's," she said.

Ben's face turned red.

"It's not what you think," he said, turning to me as the SUV pulled out of the parking lot.

"I wasn't thinking anything," I said, which wasn't entirely true.

"Jess and I are just friends," he said.

"Okay," I said, trying to sound like it didn't matter to me one way or the other. "Now come on. We're here for a reason, remember?"

We went back into the library, and Ben led me to a shelf that was filled with identically bound books—the collection of St. Mildred's yearbooks.

"You really know your way around this place," I said. I wondered just how much time he had spent in St. Mildred's library—and with whom.

"I come here every now and again," he said.

"To hang out with Jess and Stephanie?"

"To look at yearbooks. That's why I should have thought of this."

"Uh, do you mind if I ask why you'd come here to look at yearbooks?" I said.

He studied me for a moment, as if he were trying to decide if he even wanted to answer.

"My mother walked out on us when I was eight years old," he said at last. "She just packed a suitcase and left. She was sick."

"Sick?"

"Like Pete."

I couldn't imagine how it must have felt to lose someone—his mother—like that.

"I'm sorry," I said.

Ben just shrugged. "After she left, my dad threw out all of her stuff. Everything she had left behind. Her clothes, her books, pictures, her old school stuff. It was like he blamed her for being sick, you know? Then one day, a couple of years ago, I happened to be here."

"For one of those famous Ashdale–St. Mildred's social events?" I said.

"Not exactly." He hesitated. "I—I used to hang out with Jess. But it was nothing serious, and it was a long time ago. Now we're just friends." He looked anxiously at me. "Anyway, we were in here and I saw all those year-books and I was curious. So I took a look to see if there were any pictures of my mom."

"Do you know where she is now?" I asked.

Ben's eyes clouded over. "She died."

"I'm sorry."

"She died when I was ten."

"Are there any pictures?" I said.

He nodded.

"Can I see?"

He hesitated for a moment. Then he pulled a year-book from the stacks, thumbed through the pages, and held it out to me.

"That one," he said, pointing at a photograph of a young woman in a formal dress. She was wearing a tiara on her head and standing arm-in-arm with a young man wearing a crown. "She was Queen of the Prom," Ben said. His voice was soft and warm.

"She's beautiful," I said. "Actually, you look a lot like her." He shrugged modestly. "Who's the guy she's with?"

"My dad." His voice had turned cold. He closed the book and slipped it back onto the shelf. "Mr. Duffy was between about sixty and sixty-five. He might even have been a little younger—life on the street ages a person fast. So . . ." He ran his hand backward along the shelf of yearbooks. "What do you say we start here, just to be on the safe side?" He carried a pile of yearbooks to the nearest library table. He pulled out a chair for me and then sat down beside me as I leafed through the books.

Every time I set one aside, he seemed to slouch a little lower in his chair.

It didn't take long to get through each book. Most of the pictures were of girls, so I skipped those. I slowed down only when I got to the pages of photos that documented the school's co-ed activities—debate competitions, volunteer activities, fundraising events, and school dances. A lot of the pictures on those pages included boys—impossibly clean-cut, with slicked-back hair and the kind of suits that you see in old movies. I scanned each boy's face but didn't recognize any of them.

I reached for another book.

"Still nothing?" Ben said. "Are you sure you remember the picture?"

"Pretty sure," I said, paging through yet another volume.

"Talk about a long shot," Ben said. "I mean, it's not like every girl at St. Mildred's went out with a guy from St. Mark's. There wouldn't be a photo of every couple anyway. For all we know, Duffy found that ring somewhere . . ."

I heard him talking, but I wasn't really paying attention. I was too busy staring at a particular photograph— one of half a dozen on the page. It was similar to the one Ben had just showed me of his mother and father, except that the clothes worn by the young man and young woman looked even more old-fashioned. I tapped the young man's face.

"That's him," I said.

CHAPTER **FOURTEEN**

"Are you sure?" Ben said.

"Positive." I hadn't had the picture of Duffy for long, but I had studied it and studied it, trying to see his face in it. The face in that old photograph had branded itself into my brain, and I was certain I was looking at it again. The young man in this yearbook was the same young man in the small photo Aisha had given me. In the yearbook picture he was standing beside an exceptionally pretty young woman. She had eyes that held the camera, that demanded you focus on her. There was no caption under the photograph. In fact, there were no captions under any of the photos on the page.

"So close, and yet so far," Ben said.

"If she was at the prom, then she was a student here," I said. "We can find out her name, even if we can't find his."

I flipped back through the yearbook until I came to individual pictures of that year's St. Mildred's students.

"There she is," I said, pointing triumphantly. "Frances Pfeiffer."

"That's great!" Ben said with far less enthusiasm. "But what good does it do? This yearbook is—" He flipped back to the cover. "It's forty-five years old, Robyn."

"Which means that...Frances Pfeiffer is sixty-three or sixty-four. She's probably still alive." I stared at the youthful photo and tried to imagine what she might look like in the present.

"If she is, I'll bet you anything that she got married at some point and changed her name. That's what women did then. How are we going to find her?"

I thought about it while Ben made photocopies of both pictures—the one of Frances Pfeiffer alone and the one of her with the mystery boy. But it wasn't until we had replaced all the yearbooks and headed out of the library that I came up with a plan.

"That woman who gave you the brochure," I said. "What's her name?"

"Mrs. Macklin," Ben said. "Why?"

"She might be able to help us," I said.

Ben looked doubtful. "Frances Pfeiffer must have graduated at least ten years before Mrs. Macklin," he said. "They've probably never met."

"But when she was talking about raising money for the new computer lab, it sounded like she knew how to get in touch with alums," I said. "If she doesn't have an address or phone number for Frances Pfeiffer, she might know how to get one."

Ben hunted down a phone book and called Macklin. He ended up leaving a message on her voice mail.

"If she calls me back, I'll let you know," he told me. He did not sound hopeful.

.   .   .

My cell phone rang later that night.

"You were right," Ben said. He sounded slightly breathless. "You're so smart, Robyn."

"You mean Mrs. Macklin thinks she can find out where Frances Pfeiffer is?"

"Better. Frances Pfeiffer lives right here in town— she moved back from out west a couple of months ago. Her name is Frances Braithwaite now. Mrs. Macklin gave me her address and phone number. We can contact her tomorrow."

"Let's do it in person," I said. We arranged a time and place to meet.

.   .   .

The next morning Ben and I drove to an uptown neighborhood where all the houses were enormous. Ben rang the doorbell and was greeted by a voice that came through a speaker beside the door.

"Yes?" it said.

"We'd like to speak to Mrs. Braithwaite," Ben said.

"Is she expecting you?"

"No," Ben said. "But—"

The front door suddenly opened and a woman, dressed in a coat and boots, stepped out. Her car keys were dangling from one hand.

"I'm Mrs. Braithwaite," she said. She looked to be in her mid-sixties, but her eyes were still as arresting as they had been when she was a student at St. Mildred's. A startling pale blue. "But I'm on my way out, so—"

"My name is Ben Logan," Ben said. "We got your address from Mrs. Macklin at St. Mildred's." Braithwaite nodded and smiled politely, but she looked distracted. "My mother went to St. Mildred's," Ben continued. "This is my friend Robyn Hunter."

"I'm sorry," Braithwaite said, "but I really have to go."

"This will only take a minute," I said. I pulled one of the photocopied pictures from my bag, smoothed it out, and handed it to her. "Is this you?"

She fished in her handbag for a pair of reading glasses and put them on. Her pale blue eyes widened as she studied the photo.

"Where did you get this?" she said.

"From your high-school yearbook."

"Yes, I can see that. What I mean is, why? What are you doing with this picture?"

"I was hoping you could tell me who the boy is."

She looked at the picture again and her face softened. "His name was Maxwell Templeton."

"*Was?*" Ben said.

"He died a long time ago."

"Are you sure?" I said.

"Quite sure. He's been dead for twenty-two—no, twenty-three—years. Why are you—" A cell phone rang. Mrs. Braithwaite pulled one from her coat pocket. "Yes, I know," she said after a moment. "I'm on my way. I'll be there in fifteen minutes." She ended her call. "I really must go," she said. "My daughter is getting married next month and with that and Christmas . . . I'm sorry." She handed the photocopy back to me. For a moment I thought she was going to say something else, but she bustled out to the car that was parked in the driveway and drove off.

I looked down at the picture in my hand. Slowly I crumpled it into a ball and jammed it into my coat pocket.

"You did everything you could," Ben said. "More than most people would have. I guess some things just aren't meant to be."

. . .

I had just let myself into my father's loft and waved to Tara, who was in my father's office, when my cell phone rang. My heart fluttered as I checked the display. Long distance—Nick?

"Hello?" I said breathlessly.

"Hello," came a voice I didn't recognize. The caller identified himself as Doctor Antoski.

"You wanted to talk to me," he said.

I didn't know a Dr. Antoski, and I was about to tell him that he must have the wrong number when he said, "I work at the walk-in clinic on Dennison. I'm in the airport in Nairobi. I just checked my messages and there was one from you. Something about Mr. Duffy."

Then I remembered. Morgan had left a message with my cell-phone number for the doctor Mr. Duffy always saw.

"How is Mr. Duffy?" he said.

"I'm afraid he died," I said.

There was a pause on the other end.

"How did it happen?"

"He'd been drinking," I said. "They said he passed out."

"If I told him once, I told him a thousand times that it wasn't the street that was going to kill him, it was that cheap red wine that he was always drinking." The doctor sighed on the other end of the line. "I thought I'd finally got through to him. The last time I saw him, he told me he hadn't touched a drop for a couple of months. That was a big deal for someone like him."

I quickly explained why I—well, Morgan—had left the message.

"Did Mr. Duffy talk much about himself?" I said.

He seemed to hesitate. "No, not really," he said finally.

"Did he ever talk about his past?"

"Never."

"Not even about what happened to him. How he'd had that head injury?"

"I asked him a couple of times," Dr. Antoski said. "He'd had a serious blow to the head. His skull was caved in on one side. It affected the vision in his left eye, as well as some of his brain function. But he never told me anything about it. Whether he didn't like to talk about it, or he didn't remember . . . It's funny, though. Even with that, he was an expert with computers. In fact, he helped me with some problems I was having with mine. That's not something you'd expect from a man his age, let alone a person without a home. I'm sorry he's gone. And I'm sorry I can't be more help to you."

Disappointed, I thanked him and hung up. It looked like Ben was right. Some things weren't meant to be.

Tara came out of my father's office with an enormous smile, carrying what looked like a computer case.

"I finally got my computer back," she said. "And it's working! I feel like celebrating." She studied my somber expression. "You look awfully glum. Everything okay?"

"I've been working on a puzzle," I said. "I was hoping I'd solve it, but . . ." I shrugged.

"How about if I buy us coffee and a decadent dessert?" Tara said. "I know a place that has amazing brownies—à la mode, with a hot chocolate sauce to die for. What do you say?"

"Sounds good," I said with as much enthusiasm as I could muster.

My phone rang again. This time it was Aisha.

"I found something else that belonged to Mr. Duffy," she said. "Can you meet me at the laundromat?"

I said I'd be right there.

"Change of plans?" Tara said.

"I have to meet someone. I'm sorry."

"Is it going to take long?"

"I don't think so."

"Come on, then. I'll drive you to where you're going, and when you're done we'll get dessert. There's nothing like chocolate when you need a lift."

"Are you sure I'm not messing up your plans?"

"The only plan I had was to celebrate the return of my life-support system," she said. "I can't function without my computer. What do you say, Robyn? You can tell me all about your puzzle. Maybe I can help you work it out."

Tara waited in the car while I went into the laundry place. I found Aisha alone in front of a dryer.

"Rashid is at home watching Yasmin. I told him I had to do the washing early this week—the laundry will be closed on Friday for the holiday." She reached into the pocket of her thin coat and pulled out a silver locket. "I found this in Yasmin's drawer," she said. "She says Mr. Duffy gave it to her. The chain is broken. Yasmin says she didn't do it. She says it was that way when Duffy gave her the locket. He wanted her to have it, and he made her promise not to tell. He knew that Rashid would insist that she return it."

I opened the locket. There was a small oval space inside for a photo. It was empty.

"The picture I gave you," Aisha said. "I think it was originally in this locket. And look." She pointed to the locket's inside cover, opposite where the picture had been. It had been engraved: *To Franny. Eternally yours, Max.*

"The picture was of a man named Maxwell Templeton," I told Aisha. "And I'm pretty sure that *Franny* must be a woman named Frances Braithwaite. She used to know Maxwell Templeton. She told me he died more than twenty years ago."

"What was Mr. Duffy doing with it?"

"I have no idea."

"Will you return it?" Aisha said.

"Won't Yasmin be disappointed?"

Aisha looked squarely at me. "If you know who it belongs to, then please return it," she said. "It's the right thing to do. If someone had given me a locket like that, I would want it back. Wouldn't you?"

. . .

Tara took me to the dessert place and ordered lattes and a chocolate-fudge brownie with two spoons. I forced myself to eat some of it, but I think all I did was dampen Tara's celebration.

"It looks like that puzzle of yours is driving you crazy," she said finally.

"It is," I said. "I hit a dead end, and I don't like the feeling."

"I know what you mean," she said. "Why don't you tell me about it? I always feel better when I have a chance to talk things out."

I told her the whole long story.

"I was hoping the picture would turn out to be Mr. Duffy," I said, fingering the locket. "But it looks like another dead end. I should have known. The picture didn't look even remotely like him."

"Some people's faces stay perfectly recognizable," Tara said. "But you'd be surprised how much a face can change between sixteen and sixty, especially if a person is ill or had an accident or a particularly difficult life."

"Maybe," I said. "But the person in my picture turns out to have died over twenty years ago."

"Tough break," Tara said.

We finished our treat, and Tara offered to drive me home.

"I have to make another quick stop," I said. I had made a promise to Aisha. Maybe I couldn't find out any more about Duffy. But I *could* return the locket to its rightful owner—assuming she wanted it back. Her name had changed from Pfeiffer to Braithwaite, so she must have gotten married. Maybe she had thrown the locket away years ago. Still . . .

"You go ahead," I said.

"I'll take you," Tara said brightly. "It's the least I can do."

. . .

Mrs. Braithwaite's car was parked in her driveway, but I hesitated. She was probably busy. She might not be happy to see me—or the locket.

"Problem?" Tara said when I hesitated.

"No." *Just do it*, I told myself. "I don't think I'll be long."

This time Braithwaite answered the buzzer herself. When I identified myself and said that I had something of hers, she told me I must be mistaken. But when I told her it was a locket and read out the inscription, she was silent for a moment, then said, "I'll be right there."

A minute later, the door opened and she admitted me inside. I handed her the locket. She opened it and let out a sort of moan.

"Where did you get this?" she said.

When I told her, she shook her head.

"Is it possible?" she said. "Is it really possible that something you lost more than twenty years ago could suddenly turn up again, thousands of miles from where you lost it?"

"Mother?" a voice called from the hallway. "I heard the door."

A young woman who looked about Tara's age poked her head in. "Oh, I'm sorry," she said, when she saw me. A young man trailed after her. "I heard the door," the young woman said. "I thought it was Edward's father. He should have been here by now."

Braithwaite introduced me to her daughter Jenny and to Jenny's fiancé Edward. Jenny looked at her mother again.

"Is everything all right, Mother?" she said.

Braithwaite nodded weakly. "Robyn came to return this to me," she said. She handed her daughter the locket.

"The chain's broken," Jenny said.

"I did that," Braithwaite said, "just before I threw it at your father."

Jenny looked surprised. "You threw this at Daddy? I don't remember you two ever even arguing."

"Look inside, Jenny."

Jenny did as she was told. "Max?" she said. "You mean—"

"I mean your real father, Jenny."

"But he died when I was a baby."

"You were two and a half," Mrs. Braithwaite said, taking the locket back from her daughter. "It should have been the happiest time of our lives." She ran her thumb across the surface of the locket. "I didn't think I'd ever see this again," she said to me. "Max and I met when we were in school. He was at St. Mark's. I was at St. Mildred's. He was a year older than I was. He gave me this locket in my senior year. It used to have a picture of him inside."

"I know," I said. "I had the picture—and a ring from St. Mark's. That's how found you."

"You have the picture *and* his St. Mark's ring?" she asked. "May I see them?"

I explained to her that both the ring and the photograph had been stolen.

Her eyes grew misty as she looked at the locket again. "Max and I planned to get married as soon as we graduated, but my parents thought I was too young. They sent me to Europe for a year. Max went away to college. We wrote to each other for a while and then, I don't know, just drifted apart. I got married, but it didn't work out. Then one day I ran into Max. In an airport, of all places. I hadn't seen him in seventeen years. We had dinner together, and it was as if we had never been apart. We got married six months later. Two years after that, just when I thought it would never happen, Jenny came along."

"I don't understand," Jenny said. "If this is your locket, what was *she* doing with it?"

"Someone gave it to me," I said. "A woman I know asked me to return it."

"But how did she come to have it?" Braithwaite asked. "I ripped that locket off my neck and threw it at Max more than twenty years ago. That was the last time I ever saw him or the locket. How did some other woman end up with it?"

"A homeless man gave it to her," I said.

"A homeless man? Where did *he* get it?"

"I don't know."

"Well, does this woman know how to find him? Can we ask him?"

"I'm afraid not," I said. "He died last Monday night. He froze to death."

Mrs. Braithwaite stared at me.

"I just don't understand," she said. "After I threw that at Max, it was never recovered, but I assumed he had it with him when he—" She broke off suddenly, her face twisting in anguish. I felt sorry that I had come. All I had succeeded in doing was stirring up painful memories.

"My father drowned," Jenny said.

"I'm sorry," I said.

"Your father killed himself," Braithwaite said quietly.

Jenny stared at her mother. "Killed himself?" she said. "You never told me that."

"It was such a long time ago. You were so young— too young. And Steven was such a good father to you. I didn't think . . . I'm sorry. I should have told you."

Jenny looked at her fiancé, who slipped an arm around her.

"I should go," I said quietly, but no one seemed to hear me.

"After you were born," Braithwaite said, "I had a hard time coping. I was home alone a lot. And Max had changed so much in the short time we'd been married. The only thing he seemed to care about was programming and debugging. And he was drinking—far too much. He was driven by his work—at least, that's what I thought at the time.

"Max had such big ideas. He thought he could change the world. He drove himself hard. The last time I saw him, he said he was going to the office. He said he couldn't think, at home with a crying baby. That's when I yanked the locket off. The chain cut into my neck before it broke. I was so angry. I told him if work was more important than his wife and daughter, he could live at the office for all I cared. I didn't see what was really going on with him."

"What do you mean?" Jenny said.

"I found out . . . later . . . that he was being treated by a psychiatrist. He'd been drinking to deal with his depression. But he kept working. He forced himself. He kept muttering about problems at work, but he never told me what they were. He never said anything to me about how he was feeling. But I should have seen." Her eyes filled with tears.

Jenny slipped out of Edward's embrace and hugged her mother.

"His office was in a run-down place near the docks. He always said he didn't want to waste money on what he called nonessentials. You remember the place, Edward?"

Edward nodded. "I used to go there with Dad."

"Edward's father and Max were business partners," Braithwaite said. Her eyes clouded. "They found Max's watch in the harbor, his shoes and a few articles of clothing washed up. But they never found his body. They thought that maybe the tide . . . The police said there was no evidence of foul play. They knew he'd been in a bar earlier that night. At first they thought maybe he drank too much and fell into the water. When they found out he'd been seeing a psychiatrist, his death was ruled a suicide. I'm sorry, Jenny. I should have told you."

"Mrs. Braithwaite," I said hesitantly. "You said your husband worked on programming, debugging. Was he in the computer business?"

She nodded. "He'd been fascinated by computers ever since he first heard of them. This was the early days of the business. Max was a real innovator."

"Did you by any chance live out west when you were married to him?"

"Yes," she said. She gave me a curious look. "How did you know?"

I tried to tell myself it was just a coincidence. But I couldn't help thinking about what people had told me—the daffodils he'd mentioned, the computer magazines he used to read, the photo, the ring, what Tara had said about hard times changing a person's face.

"I'm pretty sure that the man who froze to death lived out west for a while. And he knew a lot about computers."

"What are you saying?" said Edward.

"I also know that he was in some kind of accident a long time ago—he'd had a serious head injury. It might've affected his memory."

Mrs. Braithwaite stared at me. "I don't understand," she said.

"You said they never found your husband's body," I said slowly. "So it's possible . . ." My voice trailed off. Was it *really* possible?

Mrs. Braithwaite's face turned pale. She stared at the locket in her hand. "It can't be," she said firmly. Then she looked up at me. "Can it?"

"I don't know," I said. "But there might be a way we can find out."

I told Mrs. Braithwaite, Jenny, and Edward about Tara.

CHAPTER **FIFTEEN**

"Do you have any photographs of Mr. Templeton before he disappeared, Mrs. Braithwaite?" Tara asked.

Braithwaite didn't answer. She still looked pale and rattled.

"I have one," Jenny said. She disappeared from the room and returned a moment later with a framed photograph. It showed a small girl smiling on the lap of a handsome man who looked like an older version of the boy in the yearbook photo. But he didn't look anything like Duffy. Maybe I had been wrong. Maybe I was upsetting this woman for nothing.

Tara examined it. "Do you have any other pictures?" she asked Mrs. Braithwaite.

Braithwaite managed to nod. "But they're still in storage back home. I moved here a few months ago, but not everything has followed me yet."

I pulled the photocopy of the yearbook picture from my pocket. Tara studied it, frowning a little. "The quality isn't very good," she said. "I don't know if I can use it." Tara looked at Braithwaite. "How about photos of any of his relatives? His father or mother. Did he have any siblings?"

"What do you need those for?" Jenny said.

"Well, say the police came to me and wanted me to age the photo of a fugitive who committed a crime, oh, thirty years ago. In the photo they give me, the person is twenty-five. If I know who the person is, I'd try to get photos of some of his relatives—brother, sister, father, mother—at age twenty-five, and then at age fifty-five, which is how old the person would be now. That gives me some idea of how the faces of people in his family change as they age and how his face might have changed."

Mrs. Braithwaite shook her head. "I don't have anything like that here."

"What about that photo Dad gave you?" Edward said to Jenny. "That might help."

Jenny hurried from the room again and returned with a second photo: two young men flanked by an older couple. I recognized one of the young men as Max Templeton.

"This is my father and Edward's father just after they graduated university," Jenny told Tara. "That's my grandparents with them."

Mrs. Braithwaite looked surprised to see the photograph. "Where did you get that?" she said.

"Edward's father brought it with him. He said he'd found it while he was cleaning out his office. He thought I'd like to have it."

"It'll be a big help," Tara said. She nodded at a tidy, antique desk. "May I set up here?"

Mrs. Braithwaite nodded. Tara unzipped her computer case, pulled out her laptop and a scanner, and set them up on the desk. She scanned the photographs that Jenny had given her.

"Can we watch you work?" I said.

Tara nodded.

We looked on in silence. I was amazed, but not surprised, when the bright-eyed young man in the original photo gradually transformed into an older, more wrinkled, and jowlier man. I glanced at Mrs. Braithwaite, who frowned at the image that was taking shape.

"Did Mr. Duffy wear glasses?" Tara asked. "Was he bald? Did he have facial hair—a beard, maybe, or a moustache?"

"I don't think he wore glasses," I said. "If he did, I never saw them. He wasn't bald. His hair was long and gray and kind of wavy. It hung down over his collar. He didn't have a beard exactly, but the times I saw him, he looked like he needed a shave."

"What about that accident he had?" Tara said. "Did it leave any permanent damage—scars, anything like that?"

"His head was caved in on one side," I said. "And he had a scar over his left eye." I used a finger to show on my own face what I meant. "The eye was deformed. It looked like it been twisted."

I heard an intake of breath beside me. Mrs. Braithwaite's lips trembled as she watched Tara adjust the images on the screen.

"Like that?" Tara said.

"The scar should be bigger," I said. "And the eye should be more scrunched up."

Tara made more adjustments until—

"That's him," I said. "That's Mr. Duffy. That's what he looked like."

"Really?" Tara sounded pleasantly surprised.

"My God," Braithwaite said. She swayed on her feet. Jenny and Edward each took one arm and lowered her into a chair. "I've seen that man before," she said. "I've dropped money in his hat. But I never spoke to him, and he never said a word. Most of the time he had his head down. Except for once. One time he looked up at me. I saw all those scars, that ravaged face. I felt so bad that I opened my purse and I gave him a twenty-dollar bill. I don't think I saw him again after that."

"When was that?"

"I don't know," she said. "A few weeks ago, I think."

Edward came over to look at the computer screen. "He looks familiar," he said.

"He always begged in front of the same office building downtown," I said. I told him which one.

"That's it," Edward said. "I saw him a couple times, just down the street from the company's new offices.

A couple of weeks ago I was going to meet Dad at a restaurant near his building. While I was crossing the street, I saw Dad drop some money into the guy's hat. The man said something to Dad." He thought a moment. "Something about a fanny. I remember thinking he must be a bit crazy."

I thought about the name engraved in the locket.

"Are you sure he didn't say Franny?" I said.

"Franny?" He started to shake his head. Then he looked at Mrs. Braithwaite and his eyes widened. "Yeah, maybe," he said. "It could have been Franny. I didn't hear clearly."

"Max used to call me Franny," Mrs. Braithwaite said. "He's the only person I've ever let call me that."

"I saw him a second time a few days later. I gave him money," Edward said. He glanced at Jenny, who was still staring at the computer screen. "I'd better call Dad," Edward said. "He'll want to hear about this."

He tried a number, then shook his head. "His phone's off. Maybe I can catch him at the hotel." He dug in his pocket, pulled out a business card, and dialed the number on it. While he waited for an answer, the doorbell rang. Jenny went to get it.

"Oh," she said, sounding surprised. "Edward was just calling you."

When she returned a moment later, a man was with her. I was as surprised to see him as he was to see me.

"Mr. Franklin," I said.

"Robyn, isn't it?" he said.

"You two know each other?" Edward said.

"I met Robyn outside the other day," Mr. Franklin said. "She was playing detective." He smiled at me. "I made a donation to your shelter."

"I heard," I said. "They were really happy about that."

"As for the rest of the matter," he said, "I've asked around the office, but I'm afraid I wasn't able to discover anything. A few people remembered the man, but nobody had spoken to him." He glanced at Tara and Edward quickly introduced her.

"Dad, *we've* just discovered something," Edward said. "At least, I think we have."

"That homeless man who froze to death," Mrs. Braithwaite said, her voice trembling. "James...we think it might have been Max."

"*Max?*" Franklin gasped. "What do you mean?"

Jenny filled him in.

"That's preposterous," Franklin said when she had finished.

He looked at Mrs. Braithwaite. His tone was softer when he spoke to her. "Frances, it can't be Max. Max is dead. This picture—" He nodded at the computer screen. "It's not even science."

"It's not *conclusive*," Tara said. "But it is pretty accurate. There are more reliable steps you can take to confirm his identity. DNA, for example."

"But his body was never found," Braithwaite said to Franklin. "What if he didn't commit suicide? What if he didn't *die*? Robyn said he had a serious head injury. What if he didn't come home because he *couldn't*? My God, what if his funeral was only last week?" Tears streamed down her cheeks.

Jenny hugged her mother tightly. "You couldn't have known."

"You can't seriously think Max has been alive all this time," Franklin said.

"Look, Dad," Edward said, turning Tara's computer around so that his father could take a good look at the screen. "We saw this man, remember? He said something to you about Franny."

"We *saw* this man?"

"You gave him money."

"Did I?" Mr. Franklin shook his head. "That cannot possibly be Max."

"There's a very good chance it is," Tara said.

"He froze to death, James," Braithwaite said. "Max froze to death. On the street. Only a few miles from where we are right now."

"Frances, we don't know anything for certain. I'm sure there are ways to find out, like this young woman said. There must be steps we can take. But really, it seems highly unlikely that that man was Max."

"But what if he was?"

"If he was, we'll deal with it. But Jenny is right— you couldn't have known. Apparently *I* dropped money into his hat and I didn't recognize him, either. Certainly no one can fault *you*, Frances. You're one of the most generous people I know. If it will make you feel better, we can keep supporting that shelter of Robyn's. You can help to make sure that no one else has to freeze to death in this city." He looked at me. "How *can* such a thing happen? How can a man freeze to death in the middle of a big city like this? It just doesn't seem right."

"According to the pathologist, Mr. Duffy had had a lot to drink that evening. He passed out with only one thin blanket over him. That's why he froze."

"Drinking?" Mr. Franklin shook his head again. "Well, that sounds like Max. He never could resist his Napoleon . . ."

That wasn't entirely true, I thought. According to Aggie and Dr. Antoski, Duffy hadn't had a drink in months. *Why did he pick the coldest night of the year to back-slide?* I wondered. I hoped it wasn't because he had been barred from the homeless shelter.

Mrs. Braithwaite wiped her tears and turned to Tara. "Who can we contact?" she said. "Who can help us prove this one way or the other?"

CHAPTER **SIXTEEN**

"I wasn't kidding," my father said. "You're a natural."
He looked up from the newspaper and beamed proudly at me. "And, if you ask me, they should have put your picture in the paper along with those pictures of Max Templeton."

The story hadn't made the front page, but it was Christmas Eve and a slow news day, so our local paper had run a longish article that described the photographic ageing that Tara had done, then detailed some of Maxwell Templeton's known history. It showed four photos of him—the two Jenny had provided, the one Tara had created, and the group photo from Art Donovan's shelter, enlarged to show a grainy image of Mr. Duffy's face after years of living on the street. The article mentioned that James Franklin was Max Templeton's former business partner and now a major shareholder, along with Frances Braithwaite, of the company he and Max Templeton had founded.

"Mrs. Braithwaite phoned me," I said. "She had some of Max's things taken from storage. Apparently somewhere in there was a box he'd got from his mother—his first pair of shoes, a silver baby cup, *and* the first tooth he ever lost. She found a private lab that will do a DNA analysis for her—although she seems pretty sure now that Mr. Duffy and Max were the same person."

My father kept right on beaming. "And she owes it all to my little girl," he said.

"It's such a sad story," I said. "Poor Mr. Duffy. He had lost so much. And to think that he and Mrs. Braithwaite actually saw each other, and she didn't even recognize him." I shook my head.

"Head injuries can be pretty dicey," my father said. "People's personalities can change dramatically. Their memory can be seriously impaired."

"You know what bothers her the most? The fact that she'll probably never know what happened to him—how he got hurt, why he never contacted her."

My father shook his head. "Some mysteries are a lot harder to solve than others."

"Mr. Franklin feels terrible that he didn't recognize Mr. Duffy either, she says. He thought Duffy was just ranting—he never made the link between the name Franny and Mrs. Braithwaite."

"Well, *you* did a good job, Robbie."

"I guess," I said. "But I feel like I only found out half of Mr. Duffy's story."

"You know what they say—half a loaf is better than none."

I glanced at my watch. "I gotta go, Dad, or I'm going to be late. Ben's waiting for me."

My father gave me a mischievous grin. "Ben again, huh?"

I shrugged, but I couldn't keep myself from smiling just a little. When I had told Ben what had happened, he had grabbed me and hugged me tightly. When he'd finally let me go, he'd looked into my eyes and said, "I was really wrong about you." And then, just like that, he'd kissed me. And I'd kissed him back. Without even thinking about it. Later, when I was in bed, I thought about Nick—about how it had felt when I was with him and how sure I had been that he loved me. But he was gone. He'd been gone for weeks. Maybe that's why, when I closed my eyes that night, I was thinking of Ben, not Nick.

"We're going to the shelter," I told my father. "Some kids are coming in to decorate a Christmas tree." And tomorrow, before Mom and Ted and I had Christmas dinner, Ben, Billy, Morgan, and I were going to serve food at the shelter.

"Will you be back for supper?"

I nodded.

"Do me a favor? Pick up some olive oil, will you? I'm all out."

"Sure," I said, then headed out.

. . .

A lot of heads turned when Ben and I arrived at the homeless shelter. Art Donovan spotted us from across the hall and strode toward us, smiling. He shook my hand and congratulated me on what I had done. So did Betty. Andrew was holding a copy of the newspaper and seemed to be studying it. He came up to me and quietly said, "That was good, what you did."

Betty asked me how I had managed to get so much information on a man as quiet as Mr. Duffy. I explained how Morgan and I had trudged all around the neighborhood, how I'd stood where Mr. Duffy would sit to gather information, how Ben and I had tracked down Frances Braithwaite . . .

"It's so weird about Mrs. Braithwaite, though," Ben said, not for the first time. "She actually gave him money but didn't recognize him."

"Same with James Franklin," I said.

"And that guy," Andrew said, nodding at the newspaper.

"What guy?" I said.

Andrew tapped James Franklin's face. "*That* guy."

"That's James Franklin," I said. "See?" I pointed to his name, which was printed in the caption under the photo. Andrew looked embarrassed. "He and Max were in business together. Max even spoke to James Franklin. But Franklin didn't recognize him."

"Max?" Andrew said. "Who's Max?"

"Max Templeton. That was Mr. Duffy's real name," I said. The headline above the photos read *Deceased man revealed as computer whiz Max Templeton*. I was beginning to realize at least one reason why Andrew was on the street.

"He gave him something else, too," Andrew said. "And Mr. Duffy shoved him away. Remember?"

"Who gave who something? What are you talking about, Andrew?" Ben said.

"Remember, Robyn?" Andrew said. "I told you I saw a man trying to give Mr. Duffy something, and Mr. Duffy yelled at him?" Andrew had mentioned it the day Morgan and I had come down to the shelter to start asking about Duffy. "That guy," Andrew said. He pointed again at James Franklin's face.

That didn't sound right. Edward had seen his father give money to Mr. Duffy, and he'd said that Mr. Duffy had mentioned the name Franny. But he hadn't said anything about Mr. Duffy yelling at him. Nor had Mr. Franklin.

"Are you sure that's the same man, Andrew?" I said.

He nodded.

"Did you see another man with him? A younger man?"

Andrew shook his head.

"I don't get it," Ben said. "Are you saying that Mr. Franklin gave Mr. Duffy money, and Duffy yelled at him?"

I thought back to what Andrew had told Morgan and me.

"Mr. Duffy collected money in a hat, right?" I said. Andrew nodded.

"But you the man you saw was trying to give Mr. Duffy something."

"He was trying to put something in his hand," Andrew said.

"You're sure?"

Another nod.

"That happened a couple of days before Mr. Duffy died, right, Andrew?" I asked.

"It was the day before you came to here for the first time," Andrew said.

"What's going on, Robyn?" Ben asked. "Is something wrong?"

"I don't know. Probably not," I said. But something was bothering me. Edward had said that he had encountered Duffy twice. But James Franklin remembered seeing Duffy only once, and he'd remembered only *after* Edward had reminded him. He hadn't volunteered that he'd seen him again. Maybe it had slipped his mind. But after that first time he would surely have remembered a face like Mr. Duffy's—especially if he'd been trying to give him something and Duffy had been resisting.

"You didn't see what he was giving him, did you, Andrew? Was it money?"

Andrew thought hard. "I don't know. That's what most people give—if they give us anything. Sometimes someone will give us food or a cup of coffee, but that guy wasn't doing that."

"Why would Mr. Duffy refuse money?" Ben said.

The question was still on my mind when Ben drove me back to my father's place later that day. He came upstairs and I introduced him to my dad, who promptly invited him to stay for supper—"Unless you're expected home," he added, "this being Christmas Eve."

Ben glanced at me.

"I can stay," he said. "Thank you."

We went into the kitchen, where my father had already started grilling chicken for his famous Cajun chicken wraps. Ben offered to help. My father handed us each a knife and gestured toward the heap of vegetables on the counter. While we washed and sliced green onions, peppers, and tomatoes, Ben and my father chatted about sports and school. They seemed to be getting along great—just like Nick and my father had. A wave of sadness and anger washed over me. But Ben was here, and Nick wasn't. And that wasn't my fault.

"Now for the salad dressing," my father said. He looked expectantly at me.

"What?" I said.

"I asked you to bring home some olive oil. Tell me you remembered, Robbie."

"Oh, no!" I gave him a distressed look. My father looked exasperated—for a split second.

"Nice try," he said. "Where is it?"

"In my bag." I went to fetch it. The two paperback novels that Duffy had bought from the library were sitting on a small table beside the door, where I had left them. I didn't even know why I'd hung onto them. I looked at the small rectangle of stiff paper that was sticking out of one of them—the business card that Duffy had been using as a bookmark. The business card of one of the best hotels in town. I pulled it from between the pages and stared at it.

"Robbie, do you think I could have that olive oil sometime before the start of the New Year?" my father called from the kitchen.

I walked slowly back to the kitchen with the card in my hand.

"Robbie?" my father said. "Are you okay?"

"This is the hotel where James Franklin is staying," I said. "His son phoned him while I was at Mrs. Braithwaite's. He had the same business card."

My father gave me a peculiar look.

"We found this card in one of Mr. Duffy's books," I said. "Remember, Ben?"

Ben nodded.

"Mr. Franklin is staying at this hotel. Edward says he saw his father give money to Duffy and heard Duffy say the name Franny a couple of *weeks* ago. Andrew—the guy I told you about from the shelter—he saw Mr. Franklin give something to Duffy a couple of days *before* he died. See? Andrew saw the two together. He saw Mr. Franklin trying to give Mr. Duffy something *after* Mr. Franklin had already seen Mr. Duffy once and *after* Mr. Duffy had mentioned the name Franny. Just *before* Mr. Duffy died. I don't think it was money, or he'd have dropped it into Duffy's hat. Andrew says he didn't do that."

"What are you saying, Robbie?"

"I'm not sure." But I was thinking fast. "What was Mr. Duffy doing with a card to the hotel where James Franklin was staying? How'd he get it unless Franklin *gave* it to him? And why would Mr. Franklin give the hotel's card to a homeless man he claimed he didn't know?"

Ben looked baffled.

"What exactly do you know about James Franklin?" my dad said.

"Not much," I admitted. "He seemed nice the first time we met him."

"The first time?" my father said. "You mean, at Mrs. Braithwaite's house?"

"No. I met him before that. Ben and I both did, two days before the funeral, when we were trying to find people who might have spoken with Mr. Duffy." I described how Mr. Franklin had approached me in front of the office building and how I'd told him all about the homeless shelter. "He made a donation," I said. "A big one."

"So he knew who you were, that you volunteered at the shelter," my father said. "And that you were trying to find out who Mr. Duffy was." He thought about that for a few moments. "After you first met James Franklin, did you notice anything unusual?"

"Like what?"

"Like maybe someone taking a special interest in you?"

I shook my head.

"What about the night you were mugged?"

That's when it hit me.

"There was this guy who showed up at the funeral," I said. "The day after Ben and I met Mr. Franklin for the first time. This man sat near me at the ceremony. I'd never seen him before." I described everything that I remembered about the man in the black hat. "He was also at the shelter the night I got mugged, when Andrew was showing the ring and the picture around. At first I thought he was a client. But then I saw him get into a car as I was leaving. What if . . ." I felt the hair stand up on the back of my neck. Then I shook my head. "He left before me. So he couldn't have followed me."

"That's not necessarily true," my father said. "James Franklin found out who you were and what you were doing two days before the funeral. Suppose he hired someone to check you out."

I was beginning to get a sick feeling in the pit of my stomach.

"If he did, that person would know that you traveled by bus. The best way I know to make someone think they're not being followed is to get out in front of them. He left before you, but I bet he was watching you at the bus stop. And I bet when you got into that taxi, he followed."

"You think he's the one who mugged Robyn?" Ben said, incredulous.

"Whoever took your purse kept the money and the ring, which makes sense. They're worth something," my father said. "They tossed everything else. We found your wallet, a few other items. But we never found that picture. You want to tell me why a mugger would keep a useless old photograph?"

I looked at my father. I knew he was thinking the same thing I was.

"Someone wanted to stop me from finding out who Mr. Duffy really was," I said.

"Could be," my father said.

"Do you remember that bottle I saw, Dad?"

My father nodded.

"What bottle?" Ben said.

I told him about the empty cognac bottle that had rolled out of the alley right beside where Billy and I had found Mr. Duffy.

"It was the Napoleon brand," I said.

"Fine stuff," my father added.

"You remember what you said, Dad? You said you'd be surprised if a homeless person could afford to buy that brand."

"It's top-of-the-line stuff. Why? What are you thinking?"

"I told Mr. Franklin that Max froze to death after passing out from too much alcohol, and do you know what he said? 'Max never could resist his Napoleon.'"

"Well, he *did* know the man," my dad said. "They started a business together. They worked together." But I could tell he was thinking it all through.

"People told Morgan and me that Mr. Duffy had quit drinking. And the doctor he used to see at the walk-in clinic said that when Duffy drank, it was cheap wine. And if the cognac he drank the night was expensive stuff . . ."

We looked at each other.

"There's one more thing, Dad," I said. "Mr. Duffy used to warm up at a place called the Black Cat Café. One of the guys who worked there let him use the phone sometimes. He said Mr. Duffy made a call from there a couple of days before he died."

"Does he know who Mr. Duffy called?"

I shook my head.

"Watch the chicken, Robbie," my father said, reaching for the phone. He talked to an old friend of his on the homicide squad. An hour later, Will Spivak came over to ask my father and me some questions.

. . .

I spent Christmas Day with my mother and had brunch with my dad at La Folie the next day—our post-split-up traditions.

The Tuesday after Christmas my father showed up at my mother's house. She was not pleased by the surprise visit.

"Relax, Patti," my father said. "I'm not staying long. I just want to talk to Robbie." He spotted me over her shoulder.

"Do you want to tell me why you didn't call me when Robyn was mugged?" my mother said.

My father glanced at me. "Robbie wanted to tell you herself," he said. "She handled herself well."

"She was *mugged*," my mother said.

"I'm fine, Mom," I said—again. I'd said it a million times already.

"I just need a minute with Robbie," my father said. He looked at me. "Will called me."

"Mom, let him come in. Please."

"Who's Will?" my mother said.

"Spivak. You remember him, Patti."

She did, because she stepped aside to let my father in out of the cold.

"You were right, Robbie," he said. "James Franklin received a phone call in his hotel room shortly after six the night Max Templeton died. Within minutes he was downstairs hailing a taxi. Will tracked down the driver and showed him some photos. The driver remembered James Franklin. He says he drove him to a liquor store and then dropped him off in front of a place called the Black Cat Café."

"Mr. Duffy used to go there sometimes," I explained to my mother and Ted.

"That's exactly what a man at the café told Will," my father said. "Turns out Mr. Duffy used the phone that night. He called James Franklin's hotel—shortly after six."

"Did the man at the café see Mr. Franklin?"

My father shook his head. "But he says Mr. Duffy was watching at the window, and he remembers seeing a cab. It was a busy night—a lot of people were in the place trying to stay warm. He didn't pay any attention to it. Mr. Duffy left right after that."

"What's this all about?" my mother said, curious despite herself.

"Sounds like a murder mystery to me," Ted said jovially.

"Max Templeton and James Franklin were business partners. Max's wife said Max was having some kind of problem at work. Then Max goes out one night, never comes back. He's presumed dead—a suicide. But he didn't die. Instead, it turns out he had a serious accident that left him with a brain injury, and he was never seen again—until more than twenty years later," my father said. "I wonder what kind of problems he was having at work."

"You think maybe that first accident wasn't an accident?" I said.

"You mean we're actually talking about a murder?" Ted said, his smile replaced by a look of astonishment.

"Could be," my father said. "Say, is that eggnog?" He headed for the dining room table where my mother had been laying out brunch.

My mother had opened her mouth to protest when Ted said, "It sure is. I was just going to pour myself one. Join me, Mac?" My mom sighed heavily.

CHAPTER **SEVENTEEN**

Ben and I spent the last day of the year at the homeless shelter, prepping food and playing cards with some of the regulars. I kept an eye out for Andrew. When I saw him come in, I excused myself from the card game.

"Hey, Robyn," he said. He started to smile and then stopped himself, as usual.

"Go ahead," I said. "Do it."

"Do what?"

"Give me a smile."

He shook his head.

"Come on, Andrew," I said.

He shook his head. "I can't."

"Why not?"

He looked down at the ground.

"Your teeth?"

He nodded without raising his head.

"Come on, smile for me. Please?"

His head came up slowly and, after a moment's hesitation, he forced a grin. As he revealed his teeth, his cheeks turned red and he looked down again.

"Teeth can be fixed, Andrew," I said.

"Getting them fixed costs money."

"Dental students are always looking for people to practice on. They don't charge much. Some of them do some free work, too, for people who can't afford it. I checked it out for you, found someone who'd help you out. I can make an appointment, if you'd like."

This time he did smile, widely and spontaneously. He started to cover his mouth again, but I pushed back his hand.

"Thanks, Robyn," he said.

"Happy New Year, Andrew," I said. Maybe after his teeth were fixed and he had a little more confidence, we could work on his reading problem.

At five o'clock Ben and I headed over to my dad's place to help set up for his annual New Year's Eve party. Morgan and Billy were planning to come, as were some of my father's tenants and business associates, and practically everyone else he knew.

The buzzer sounded while my father and Ben were hanging up a *Happy New Year* banner.

"Get that, will you, Robbie?" my father said.

It was Frances Braithwaite.

"I'm sorry," she said when she saw the decorations. "I don't want to interrupt. I just wanted to tell you in person—"

My father scrambled down from a stepladder and introduced himself.

"We spoke on the phone," he said. He turned to me. "Will gave Mrs. Braithwaite my number. She asked if she could drop by to see you." He waved her inside. "Can I offer you something to drink, Mrs. Braithwaite?"

"Please, call me Frances," she said. "Mr. Hunter—"

"Mac," my father said.

Mrs. Braithwaite smiled, but there was sadness in her eyes. "Mac. I just wanted to thank you and your daughter for everything. James . . ." She hesitated and drew in a deep breath. "The police have arrested James for Max's murder."

So I had been right—Mr. Duffy's death wasn't an accident. I glanced at my father but couldn't tell what he was thinking.

"The prosecutor offered to reduce the charge from first-degree to second-degree, with eligibility for parole after ten years if he confessed," Braithwaite said.

"Ten years?" I said. It didn't seem like much after what he had done. "Did he take it?"

She nodded. "James is sixty-three years old. If he were convicted of first-degree murder, he'd have spent the rest of his life in prison. At least this way he has a chance of getting out before he dies."

My father nodded but didn't say anything. Mrs. Braithwaite continued.

"James told the police that he thought he'd killed Max twenty-three years ago," she said.

"But why?" Ben asked. "What did he have against Mr. Duffy—I mean, Mr. Templeton?"

"Max and James were in business together. They did very well, made a lot of money. Then Max developed a new program that would have made them even more money—a *lot* more. But Max didn't care about that part. I remember him telling me that if money was all he was interested in, he could have already retired. He wanted to make sure that anyone who wanted to use his new program could have it."

"And Mr. Franklin didn't like that," I said.

"No, he didn't," Mrs. Braithwaite said. "He says he tried to reason with Max. But Max was having problems by then. He was deeply depressed, and he was drinking. He threatened to break up the partnership and take his new program with him."

"Is that why Mr. Franklin killed him?" Ben said.

"He couldn't bear the thought of Max giving away something that was so valuable. The last night I saw Max, we had a big fight. Max said he was going to the office. He had set up the business near the docks, where rent was cheap. The area was surrounded by warehouses. James was waiting for him. He clubbed Max with a piece of pipe, then removed his IDs, some of his clothing."

"He obviously overlooked a few items," my father said. "The locket and the ring."

"He said he heard someone coming and panicked. He dumped Max's body in a truck behind one of the warehouses. The truck was taking a shipment south, across the border. He hid Max at the very back, under some old packing blankets. Then he threw some of Max's things into the water."

"So it'd look like a suicide," my father said.

"Where did Mr. Duf— Mr. Templeton end up?" Ben said.

"No one knows," Mrs. Braithwaite said. "I'm going to hire someone to see if I can find out. All I know at this point is that Max suffered massive head trauma. He may have had brain damage, some loss of memory." She shook her head. "If only I had known. If only he had found some way to contact me."

"It must have been a shock to Mr. Franklin to run into Max after all these years," I said.

"It was," Braithwaite said. "He thought Max had been dead for years. He says he didn't even recognize him. Max spoke first. He told James that he'd seen me. Even then James didn't recognize him. To him, Max was just some homeless man. Then James saw the locket. He tried to take it."

"No wonder Max gave it to Yasmin," I said. "And he told Aisha that he was afraid the ring would be stolen."

"James said he was thunderstruck. He says he looked at him again and started to see how it could be Max. Max even had his old school ring. And then Edward came along, and James hustled him away before Max could say anything else."

"But Edward heard him say your name," I said.

"Which meant nothing to Edward. He's always known me as Frances, not Franny. And he would never have recognized Max." Mrs. Braithwaite's voice trembled.

"Let me get you some water, Frances," my father said gently.

Mrs. Braithwaite shook her head. "No, but thank you."

"Why didn't Mr. Franklin just avoid Mr. Templeton?" Ben said. "Why did he kill him?"

"Fear," Braithwaite said. "Max had mentioned my name. He had the locket. He'd said he'd seen me. He said something about wanting to go home."

"He said something like that to Aisha," I said. "Asked her if she would take him back. She didn't know what he was talking about. But maybe he was talking about *you*. Maybe he was wondering if you'd take him back after all these years, after everything that happened."

Braithwaite's eyes were misty as she nodded. "James was also afraid that someone would find out what he did all those years ago. He kept an eye on Max for the next little while."

"And then he killed him," Ben said.

Mrs. Braithwaite nodded. "James tried to get friendly with Max so that he could try to find out what Max remembered."

"He gave Max a card from the hotel where he was staying," I said. "Did he say why?"

"For the same reason," Braithwaite said. "If Max contacted him, that would mean he really did remember something—that he really did want to go home. When

Max didn't contact him, James started to think that everything was going to be okay."

"But he did call," I said. "He called the night he died."

"He was cold. He wanted a place to stay. So he called James. And that's when James saw his chance. He arranged to meet Max. On the way, he picked up a bottle of Max's favorite drink."

"The cognac," I said.

Braithwaite nodded again. "He told Max it was just a short walk to the hotel. He said he'd brought something to keep them warm on the way. He kept Max drinking until he passed out. It couldn't have taken long, with Max in the shape he was. Then James left him in a doorway and watched him for a while from across the street." She wiped tears from her eyes. "He was also responsible for what happened to you, Robyn. When he heard what you were doing, he had you followed."

By the man in the black hat.

"When he found out you had that photo, he was afraid that someone—me, I suppose—might recognize the man in it. He paid someone to take it away from you. I'm sorry. But he's given the police the man's name. If they can find him, they'll arrest him for robbery and assault."

I didn't know what to say.

"Well, at least I know what happened to poor Max," Mrs. Braithwaite said. "And I know because someone—you, Robyn—cared enough about a stranger to try to put a human face on him. I'll always be grateful for that."

"It was Ben's idea," I said.

"But Robyn did all the work," Ben said. He slipped an arm around me. My father raised an eyebrow.

"You both deserve a lot of credit," my father said. "Are you sure I can't tempt you with some eggnog, Frances?"

"Jenny and Edward are waiting for me," she said. "Poor Edward—he's shattered by what his father did. But Jenny is standing by him. And Edward is going to carry on with the business."

.   .   .

After Mrs. Braithwaite left we finished the party preparations. It wasn't long before guests started to arrive. My dad, being my dad, put on some old rock records—and a lot of Motown—and managed to get almost everyone up and dancing.

When it was nearly midnight, Ben looked around. The music was quieter as everyone started to anticipate the countdown to the New Year. Morgan and Billy swayed to the song that was playing and gazed dreamily into each other's eyes. I spotted Vern and his girlfriend Henri with their arms around each other.

"Fun party," Ben said. He looked around, maybe to check where my dad was—on the far side of the living room with a couple of cop friends. Then he pulled me into the kitchen where we were shielded from view, pulled me in close, and kissed me. The party sounds disappeared. All I heard was my heart beating in my chest. All I felt was the warmth of Ben's arms around me. Then I heard my father's booming voice.

"Look who's finally here!" he was saying. "Tara! Come in, come in."

A few moments later Tara appeared in the kitchen. Ben and I jumped apart as if we'd both been jolted with a cattle prod. Tara giggled.

"Sorry," she said. "If there'd been a door, I would have knocked. I was just looking for something to toast the New Year with."

When I introduced her to Ben, she gave me a furtive thumbs-up.

"Oh, hey, did you get that package, Robyn?" she said.

"Package?"

"A package came addressed to you. I had to sign for it. I left it—" She paused to think. "On top of the fridge!" she said, spinning around. "And there it is."

The package was a small box wrapped in brown paper. My name and my dad's address were printed neatly on it, but there was no return address.

"Open it," Ben said.

I tore off the paper and lifted the lid off the box. Nestled inside was a gold pendant in the shape of two intertwined hearts.

"Hey," Ben said. "Don't tell me you have a secret admirer!"

I laughed. "As if you didn't know what it was!"

"I didn't," Ben said. "It's not from me."

I laughed again.

"Really, Robyn," he said. "It's not from me."

I got a strange feeling.

I turned the pendant over. The engraving on the back read *To RH. Love you forever. ND.*

Nick.

"So?" Ben said, smiling. "Who's it from? Do I have a reason to be jealous?"

I put the pendant back into the box and closed the lid. "No," I said. "You don't."

CHECK OUT THE NEXT BOOK IN THE
ROBYN HUNTER MYSTERIES SERIES:

SHADOW OF DOUBT

I looked into the box. It contained a dozen red roses. Nestled among them was a baby doll. It was splattered with what looked like blood but was probably red paint. Its head was missing. I lifted it out of the box and gingerly poked among the thorns.

ROBYN HUNTER MYSTERIES

#1 *Last Chance*

Robyn's scared of dogs—but she agrees to spend time at an animal shelter anyway. Robyn learns that many juvenile offenders also volunteer at the shelter—including Nick D'Angelo. Nick has a talent for troublemaking, but after his latest arrest, Robyn suspects that he might be innocent. And she sets out to prove it . . .

#2 *You Can Run*

Trisha Hanover has run away from home before. But this time, she hasn't come back. To make matters worse, Robyn blew up at Trisha the same morning she disappeared. Now Robyn feels responsible, and she decides to track Trisha down . . .

#3 *Nothing to Lose*

Robyn is excited to hang out with Nick after weeks apart. She's sure he has reformed—until she notices suspicious behavior during their trip to Chinatown. Turns out Nick's been doing favors for dangerous people. Robyn urges him to stop, but the situation might be out of her control—and Nick's . . .

#4 *Out of the Cold*

Robyn's friend Billy drags her into volunteering at a homeless shelter. When one of the shelter's regulars freezes to death on a harsh winter night, Robyn wonders if she could've prevented it. She sets out to find about more about the man's past, and discovers unexpected danger in the process . . .

#5 *Shadow of Doubt*

Robyn's new substitute teacher Ms. Denholm is cool, pretty, and possibly the target of a stalker. When Denholm receives a threatening package, Robyn wonders who's responsible. But Robyn has a mystery of her own to worry about: What's with the muddled phone message she receives from her missing ex-boyfriend Nick?

#6 *Nowhere to Turn*

Robyn has sworn that she's over Nick. But when she hears he needs help, she's too curious about why he went missing to say no. Nick has been arrested again, and the evidence doesn't lean in his favor. When Robyn investigates, she discovers a situation more complicated than the police had thought—and more deadly . . .

ABOUT THE AUTHOR

Norah McClintock is the author of several mystery series for teenagers, and a five-time winner of the Crime Writers of Canada's Arthur Ellis Award for Best Juvenile Crime Novel. McClintock was born and raised in Montreal, Quebec. She lives in Toronto with her husband and children.